WILD RESCUERS
GUARDIANS
OF THE
TAIGA

And don't miss
Wild Rescuers: Escape to the Mesa

WILD RESCUERS
GUARDIANS
OF THE
TAIGA

Stacy Hinojosa aka *Stacy Plays*

ILLUSTRATED BY *Vivienne To*

HARPER
An Imprint of HarperCollinsPublishers

Photos on pages 194–196 are courtesy of the author
Photos on pages 197–201 are courtesy of Saranda Oestreicher;
credit to Casey McFarland

Library of Congress Control Number: 2018933332
ISBN 978-0-06-279638-7
Typography by Jessie Gang
19 20 21 22 23 PC/BRR 10 9 8 7 6 5 4 3 2 1
❖
First paperback edition, 2019

For my mom

CONTENTS

WILD RESCUERS
GUARDIANS
OF THE
TAIGA

THE TAIGA

the rabbit
rescue

the forest of
perpetual darkness

the patrol ridge

our cave

the farm

the village

taiga forest

NORTH

the wild wolf den

the ravine

the abandoned
mineshaft

stacy's farm

Stacy

Everest

Wink

Basil

Tucker

Addison

Noah

Page

Dusky

The
Wolf Pups

The Bats

Fluff & Crow

Rabbit

Fawn

Moose

WILD RESCUERS
GUARDIANS
OF THE
TAIGA

ONE

STACY LAY ON her back and stared straight into the eyes of the giant white wolf looming above her. The wolf's eyes were fixed fiercely on hers. Suddenly, his sharp teeth sliced into the sleeve of her denim jacket, narrowly missing her left arm, and pinning her to the ground.

How do I keep getting myself into these wild predicaments? Stacy thought to herself.

To complicate matters, the upper half of her body was dangling off a cliff. And immediately to her right, a small rushing stream flowed off the cliff into a narrow waterfall that thundered thirty feet into a pool of white water in the river below.

But Stacy's thoughts weren't focused on the wolf. Or on the steep drop and the water beneath her. They were focused on a rabbit.

Just out of her reach, down the jagged cliff side, on a sturdy branch poking out of the rushing falls, a baby bunny sat shivering. One small movement and the rabbit would fall from its precarious perch to its death in the water below.

I've been in worse situations . . . I think, Stacy thought. *I can do this.*

She tilted her head back to get a better look at the bunny: it was white with black spots and its little ears were flopped in front of its eyes—either because it didn't want to face the reality of its dangerous situation or because the mist from the waterfall had plastered them there. In an attempt to reach it, Stacy tried swinging her right arm down behind her. But the small creature was still a few feet from her fingertips.

She turned her attention back to the angry wolf, who had not loosened his grip on her jacket sleeve.

"It's okay, Everest," Stacy said calmly.

The large wolf replied with a low, rumbling growl.

"If you relax your hold just a tiny bit, I can lean far enough to grab it . . . probably."

Once again, the wolf growled a warning.

"Let me go, Everest," Stacy said, more firmly this time. Everest didn't often respond to commands—even though Stacy knew he understood them—but she had to try anyway. "I can do it," she insisted.

The wolf shook his head. His eyes had a pleading look. If he could talk, Stacy knew what he would say to her: "It's my job to keep you safe."

And it's my job to rescue this bunny, Stacy thought. *And that's exactly what I'm going to do.*

The mental exchange between them lasted only a few seconds, but it gave Stacy the time she needed to think over the rescue in her mind. Everything would depend on perfect precision and split-second timing.

Finally, she had her plan.

"Fine," she said, and watched the wolf back off.

Then, with a grin: "You can keep the jacket, Everest— I didn't want it to get wet anyway."

Everest's silver eyes flashed as he realized what Stacy was about to do. But he was too late.

In one fluid motion Stacy wriggled out of her jacket, rolled into the stream, and flipped around just as she slid over the edge into the waterfall. As she fell, her hands reached for (and thankfully found) the slick branch with the bunny. She grabbed the branch with one hand and scooped up the baby rabbit with the other, sheltering it against her chest while her feet found footing on the wet rocks behind the falls. Water pounded on her back, spraying in all directions, while she struggled to maintain her position. She looked around, frantically searching for a way back onto the mountain. But she quickly realized there was nowhere to go but down.

Stacy tucked the bunny underneath her well-worn blue-and-white-striped shirt, a castoff from some careless camper who'd left it behind in the woods where Stacy lived.

"Noah!" she shouted. "Are you ready?"

She waited for the sound of a bark or a howl from below, but she was met only with the deafening noise of the falls. Her feet were beginning to slip and her fingers were having trouble holding on to the slimy branch.

"I hope rabbits know how to hold their breath," she whispered to the little creature.

Stacy inhaled deeply, closed her eyes, and leapt.

She crossed both arms across her chest, hugging the rabbit close to her as the two of them plunged into the swirling rapids. After crashing through the surface, Stacy opened her eyes underwater. Unfortunately the churning made it impossible for her to see which way was up. She blew a little bit of air out of her mouth and watched the bubbles float away to her left. *Ah, that way.*

But even kicking as hard as she could, she was stuck in the circular current where the waterfall cascaded into the river. If only she'd been able to jump several feet out from the waterfall rather than straight down.

Relax, she told herself. *Noah's coming. Don't panic; if you do, you'll drown.*

With her last bit of air, Stacy pressed her lips to the bunny's tiny mouth and blew into its lungs, trying to keep it alive. And then she did what she'd told herself to do: she relaxed, sinking further into the pool, down below the rapids.

Suspended in the dark blue green water underneath the churning waves, she started to count in her head.

One . . . two . . . three . . . four . . .

She hadn't yet reached five when she felt a large jaw close around her shoulder. The wolf's grip was tight— tight enough to pull her to the surface and then proceed to maneuver her downriver, where the water was calm.

With her head above the surface, Stacy gulped in the crisp spring air and felt her lungs burn with oxygen. Then she checked the bunny. It was stunned and shivering, but still alive.

"Cutting it a little close there, Noah," Stacy said teasingly to the giant white wolf paddling beside her.

She plopped the sopping wet rabbit on top of Noah's

head. The bunny started to blink the water out of its eyes and then looked down in wide-eyed terror at the white wolf's snout. "No, you didn't go through all that just to be wolf dinner," Stacy said, hoping it would understand her. "You're safe now."

Stacy and Noah paddled together to the riverbank and stumbled onto the shore. The thin vine Stacy usually used to tie her long brown curls into a side braid had been lost in the waterfall, and now her hair was a tangled mess. She combed it using her fingers and then wrung out the bottom of her shirt and rolled up her wet jeans.

Noah lowered his head next to a large rock and the bunny hopped off, clearly relieved but still slightly shaky. Stacy scooped it up.

"You're okay, little bun," she cooed, cradling it in her arms. She turned the bunny over to inspect it and make sure it was unharmed. "And you've got quite the story to tell your friends." The bunny stared blankly back at her. "Now repeat after me: 'I will not jump down waterfalls.'"

Noah shook his entire body, spraying water droplets in all directions. They looked like tiny diamonds in the sunlight. Stacy laughed and ran her fingers through his damp coat. Then she tousled the messy tuft of fur between his ears and stared into his intense blue eyes.

"You're definitely getting better at diving, boy," she told him. "We were in there pretty deep. You got to us just in time."

Noah puffed up his chest with pride.

A short bark—one Stacy knew well—rang out from the trees behind them.

"That'll be Everest," Stacy explained to the bunny, "who's very mad at me."

The white wolf, with flecks of silver and gray in his coat and as formidable as the Himalayan peak he was named after, had descended the mountain. And he wasn't alone. There were at least a dozen rabbits hopping all around him, moving so fast Stacy didn't even try to count them individually. Everest had Stacy's jacket clenched between his teeth. He was trying to look stern, but that was impossible to pull off with a bunch of adorable rabbits darting between his legs.

Stacy burst out laughing. She gave the rescued rabbit one last gentle scratch behind its ear and placed it down on the forest floor. "Okay, then, get out of here," she said.

The bunny hopped over and caught up with the others, nuzzling noses with a large white rabbit—likely its mom or its dad—and then they all scampered into the birch trees, putting as much distance between themselves and the wolves as they could.

"You're welcome!" Stacy yelled after them. "Stay away from cliffs!"

She turned back to Noah and Everest, ignoring Everest's harsh stare. "Well, that's that," she said, taking her jacket from the wolf's mouth. She threw it around her shoulders, only now realizing how cold the water had been. She pulled her wet hair into a loose ponytail, leaving one strand of it to the side to wrap around and hold the rest in place. For all the time she spent in the forest, Stacy's skin had just enough of a hint of olive to prevent her from getting burned, although the sun had drawn out a few freckles under her green eyes, across her nose and cheeks.

"Ugh, that bunny was so cute," she said to Everest and Noah, who were both taking a drink from the river. "To be honest, I would have liked to bring it home as a pet."

Everest lifted his head and shot her a disapproving look.

"I know, I know," Stacy said with a smile. "And you would have liked to have rabbit stew for dinner. You know we don't eat our rescues, though—ever."

Everest shook his head, and Stacy could tell he was still a little disgruntled. Not about the rabbit stew (or lack of rabbit stew), but about Stacy's daring move back on the cliff. She looked into his icy-gray eyes. "I know you think I took too big a risk," she said, kneeling down beside Everest. She took several canteens out of the old leather satchel she carried with her, the original reason for their excursion to the river, and began filling them. "You know I couldn't leave that rabbit there once we'd spotted it. And I knew Noah had my back. I wouldn't have jumped otherwise."

Stacy could sense that Everest thought she went too far with some of her animal rescues, but she only did what she felt she had to do.

How do I make you understand that this is what I'm here for? I have to rescue these animals, just like you and the other wolves rescued me.

It was a point they would never entirely agree on. But they cared about each other and wanted to keep each other safe—that's what really mattered.

"C'mon, let's go home," Stacy said. "We've got a pretty decent-size walk ahead of us."

Everest led the way through the cool birch forest with Stacy in the middle and Noah bringing up the rear, still shaking water out of his ears.

Stacy took a deep breath in through her nose, the sharp spring air filling her lungs. *The forest is coming alive again,* she thought. *Getting ready for this burst of new life and . . .* AH-AAHH-ACHOOO! *. . . unfortunately, the start of my allergies.*

Allergies aside, Stacy always loved this time of year in the forest. And, even though her muscles were aching from her hike up the mountain, she was enjoying the long trip home with Everest and Noah, alternating between a brisk walk and an invigorating jog.

The bright green new leaves of the birch trees were just starting to give way to the jade-green needles of the pine and spruce trees of the taiga forest when Stacy stopped short. Something was lurking in the dark shadows of the dense trees.

A pair of yellow eyes glowed back at her.

TWO

STACY RECOGNIZED THOSE yellow eyes. "Baaaay-ziillll!" she shouted, lingering over every syllable of one of her favorite names. It was Basil, a female in Stacy's wolf pack.

Basil was the pack's beta, which meant she was second-in-command. Stacy was never quite sure whether Everest was the alpha or if *she* herself held that title. While Everest was the pack's leader in some matters, Stacy took on the role in others. It was an unusual arrangement—not least of all because Stacy was human—but they were an unusual pack and it worked for them.

Basil, slender and athletic, emerged from the trees and

sidled up beside Stacy. Named after the purple flowering wild basil plants she could often be found nibbling on, Basil was pure white and had beautiful citrine eyes.

"Hi, girl, how are you?" Stacy asked, running her hand along Basil's sleek back. Basil crouched low to the ground, letting Stacy know she could climb on.

"I'll see you two back at the cave," Stacy said over her shoulder to a tired-looking Everest and Noah as she gently swung her leg over Basil's back.

Basil took off, trotting through the taiga in the direction of their home. Stacy lowered her chest onto Basil's upper back and wrapped her arms around the wolf's broad shoulders, a signal to Basil that she could go faster.

Basil was the fastest runner in the pack—so fast that, as the wolf broke into a sprint, the trees were reduced to a green blur punctuated occasionally by the silvery bark of birch and larch trees. Stacy closed her eyes and laid her head to one side against Basil's soft neck. She was exhausted from the day's difficult rescue, but she always found peace in the familiar rhythm of the wolf's steady gait.

Stacy had no idea how she'd come to live in the taiga with six Arctic wolves. There was a fuzzy memory of a burning smell, and when she'd woken up in the middle of the forest surrounded by a pack of wolves, she had a throbbing headache. Every time she tried to recall how exactly she'd ended up so deep in the taiga forest or who she'd been with, it was like trying to close her hand around a curl of smoke—nothing.

But as emotional as that day had been, her memories of it were not bad ones. She had felt only the wolves' warmth and concern. She remembered tall, regal Everest standing watch over them all while Tucker, a white male wolf with a very thick coat, licked a gash on her knee. Basil and Addison, the other female in the pack, lay on either side of her and she was nestled into their warm fur. As tears rolled down her cheeks, Noah brushed them away with his wet nose. He pushed something toward her—a fish he'd caught in a nearby stream and somehow managed to skin and clean for her. Stacy ate it while Wink, the youngest member of the pack, sat nearby, a perplexed and curious look on his face. Wink was just a pup back then.

When the six wolves found her, Stacy had a pretty impressive vocabulary for a girl so young. Whatever the accident had been, it seemed to have erased all her memories of her family, friends, and school without affecting her intelligence one bit. She loved reading and writing. She also had a passion for nature and animals and already knew quite a bit about the wildlife that was suddenly all around her. She guessed she was around eight years old when it happened. Four winters had passed since that remarkable October morning, so Stacy figured she must be about twelve.

Now, as Basil raced through the forest with Stacy on her back, Stacy turned to one of her most common (and painful) trains of thought, pressing on it like a bruise: What had happened to her humans? She had to have had a mother and a father—but where were they now? She had seen animals abandon their young in the forest. When that happened, it was almost always because the mother didn't think they would survive. But Stacy hadn't been ill. When the wolves found her, even though she was hurt, she was healthy and well fed. She had clearly been loved, that much she knew.

Where are they, these humans who'd taken such good care of me? Stacy wondered. *Did they lose me? Did they come looking for me? . . . Have they given up?* She'd considered going to look for her parents before, many times. And she knew where she'd start—a small village bordering the western boundary of the taiga. Stacy figured if she asked enough of the villagers there, she eventually *could* find her parents. But since she had no memories of them, she wasn't entirely sure she *wanted* to find them.

Notwithstanding the occasional wonderings about her parents, Stacy loved her life in the taiga with her wolf pack. She had seen humans plenty of times in the forest and, from what she'd witnessed, their world wasn't very appealing to her. There were the heartless hunters with their guns and bows who threatened to kill the animals she loved. There were troubled teens who threw rocks at squirrels and birds, and careless campers who had no respect for the forest and left their campsites littered with garbage. Sometimes that garbage was useful in the form of old clothes or books, but too often Stacy found herself cleaning up after them when they left the woods. And once—one terrible spring—a construction company had come with big land-clearing machines and many animals had lost their homes when it flattened a chunk of the forest to create a small electrical substation. It was uglier than anything Stacy had ever seen. Its chain-link fences, messy cables, and metal towers were a blight on the beautiful forest she had come to call home.

Stacy gripped Basil's fur, relieved that the substation was a decent distance from their cave, and buried her head deeper in the thick pelage of the wolf's neck.

After about ten minutes of running, Stacy opened her eyes. Basil had slowed down enough that the individual trees and even the grayish-green lichen on their trunks came back into focus. Stacy recognized the familiar part of the taiga where she and the pack lived. Behemoth spruce trees and tall ferns dominated the landscape and continued up onto a ridge before them. Tiny brown and red and white spotted mushrooms sprung up between the fallen pine needles that covered the forest floor. And a giant moss-covered boulder marked the entrance to a small clearing in front of the ridge where the entrance to the cave Stacy and the wolves called home was nestled.

Stacy was just climbing off Basil's back when Tucker bounded out of the cave and knocked Stacy to the mushy ground. She lay back on a soft bed of brown podzol topped with orangey pine needles and green moss and reached up to pet his super-soft white fur.

"I missed you too, boy!" Stacy said with a laugh.

Addison was on his heels. She was a graceful wolf with a slight brownish tint to her light coat. She greeted Stacy by nuzzling her nose and then dropped a newspaper beside her.

Stacy laughed again. "I'm going to pretend you didn't sneak into the village to steal this off someone's porch, Addi," she said.

Addison eyed her with an innocent expression, but couldn't hold it for long. A mischievous look washed over her face before she darted away. Addison, the brainiest of the pack, had always seemed to be the wolf most concerned with Stacy's education. Addison was constantly turning up with books and newspapers she'd "borrowed" from who knows where. Once, Addison had lurked behind the small library in the village as they were thinning their shelves to make room for new books. Together, she and Stacy returned to the village in the middle of the night and gathered as many books as they could from the recycling bin where they'd been discarded. Stacy had a full library, ranging from picture books to novels like *Charlotte's Web* and—her favorite— *Island of the Blue Dolphins.* There were history books and science journals that taught her about the world. There was even a camping cookbook that Stacy and Addison had looked at together and used to test some recipes.

Addison was curiously clever for a wolf and had a proclivity for arithmetic. Stacy would never forget the summer spent in a clearing near their cave home with Addison, who carefully watched Stacy use a stick to practice her multiplication tables in the soft dirt. Stacy figured she was likely the only girl in the world who could rightfully claim she'd been homeschooled by a pack of wolves.

Stacy carried the newspaper into their cave and laid it on a large wood table in the center, one she'd crafted herself from a spruce that had been split in two and had fallen over in a storm last summer. She had used the sharp edge of a rock to smooth its surface into a dull shine. A slightly charred loaf of bread she'd baked the day before sat on top. She cut two slices using a knife left behind by some campers and slathered it with peanut butter—another one of Addison's illegal acquisitions.

I have to talk to her about that, Stacy thought. *If too many things disappear, the villagers will start looking for the thief. And if they search the taiga, they might find me. I'd have to leave the forest and I'd never see the wolves again.*

She shook away those thoughts and walked over to

a small waterfall in one of the back corners of the cave. She reached her hand through the trickling stream to the cool ledge behind it and felt around until her hand clasped a small glass jar of blackberry jam she had made from the berries that grew wild in the forest. The cold stream of water made for a perfect refrigerator.

Stacy slathered the jam on the other slice of bread and pressed the two sides together to make a sandwich before wandering over to the cave's fireplace. There was a huge rocking chair next to it—another one of Stacy's projects, one long winter afternoon. Curved branches served as rockers, and she'd used sharp rocks as saws and sandpaper (again, she really needed to talk to Addison about her thievery) to make the planks for the seat, back, and arms. It was all held together with strong vines and even stronger glue made from pinesap.

Stacy sat down with the newspaper in one hand and her sandwich in the other while Basil was busy starting a fire in the massive stone hearth with a flint and steel. Fire starting was, Stacy had to admit, a rather peculiar skill for a wolf, but Basil was no ordinary wolf. None of them were.

Stacy unfolded the newspaper to read the front page. The biggest headline immediately caught her attention.

VILLAGE COUNCIL TO ADDRESS WOLF PROBLEM, POSSIBLE BOUNTY

The wolf population in the taiga forest on the edge of the village is on the rise. Three area farmers have lost livestock in recent weeks leading to calls for a wolf bounty to thin the growing population of predators.

"The wolves are a menace," said villager Orrin Webster. "In the last month alone, I've lost two sheep and a cow to wolves."

"The wolves in the forest have no natural predator," added Amos Sheridan, who found the carcasses of two of his sheep on the edge of the forest three days ago. "They've depleted their natural food sources and have turned on our flocks. It has to stop."

Both men pointed to a solution the village enacted nearly twenty years ago: a wolf bounty. Hunters were paid a bounty of fifty dollars for each wolf pelt they produced. After a year, the wolf population had decreased significantly and the bounty was withdrawn. That program was considered a success by both the farmers and the village council.

"Hmmm, it's an interesting idea," said village councilwoman Elna Meyers. "The local farmers have asked us to consider reinstating a wolf bounty, and that's what we'll be looking at carefully in the coming weeks. We have to weigh all the factors and invite people on both sides of the issue to come forward."

The council will hold its first meeting to discuss the issue on Monday in the Village Hall.

Stacy suddenly felt a heavy weight on her chest. She took a huge bite of her sandwich and read the headline again. *Her* wolves weren't the problem, that much she knew. A small pack of Great Plains wolves—a breeding pair and a couple of juveniles—had moved into their part of the taiga a few summers ago. Their numbers had been steadily increasing ever since. Everest and Basil had both been anxious from the moment the new pack arrived, but the two packs had established an uneasy truce. As much as Stacy wished the wild wolf pack would move on to new territory, she didn't want her wolves to purposely try to drive the others away.

They must have been the ones who killed the villagers' livestock. But why? It wasn't like the wild wolves didn't have full run of the forest. Stacy and her pack were rescuers—they didn't hunt. They subsisted mainly on Noah's daily fish catches and Stacy's small garden, leaving all the forest's large mammals for the wild wolves' diet. As much as Stacy hated it, she understood wolves were carnivores and needed to eat. They must have increased their hunting radius to include the farmers' fields. And now that they'd tasted mutton, it was only a matter of time before they killed more sheep in the village.

Stacy frowned and began furiously picking blackberry seeds out of her teeth. If the council passed the bounty, hunters wouldn't discriminate between Stacy's pack and the wild wolves—they would all be in danger. She didn't want to worry the others, but when Everest returned she'd tell him what she'd learned. Maybe he could persuade the other pack to go farther north to a new hunting ground. Then the whole thing might blow over.

Stacy ripped the article out of the newspaper and tucked it into her pants pocket. She couldn't risk the wolves finding out before she'd talked to Everest. She wasn't sure if Addison had managed to teach herself how to read, but Stacy wouldn't put it past her.

Stacy had just started to eat the second half of her sandwich when she realized that something, or rather, someone, was missing.

"Hey, has anyone seen . . ."

Before Stacy could even finish her question, that someone appeared. It was his wagging tail that Stacy saw first. *Wink!* Wink backed into the cave, his rear end leading the way. Wink's normally white fur, which puffed out in all directions, was a dull, dirty gray. Stacy made a mental note to bring him to the river the next time she went and give him a bath. His butt was sticking up in the air, his head was lowered, and he seemed to be dragging something that required all his focus.

Wink worked his way backward through the cave until Stacy could see what he was dragging. His jaw was clenched firmly around the handle of a bucket brimming with frothy white liquid.

"Milk!" Stacy exclaimed, jumping to her feet from the rocking chair.

As he drew closer, the milk sloshed over the edge of

the bucket and dripped onto the ground.

"Oh, Wink! Did you take that from a farmer? How did you manage to get it all the way . . ."

Wink tried turning toward her, losing even more milk over the side of the bucket.

"No, just set it dow—"

It was too late. The bucket teetered to one side. Milk spilled everywhere. Wink slipped, each of his four paws sliding out from under him in a different direction, leaving him flat on his belly with his snout in a puddle

of milk. Wolves don't blush, but Stacy could tell how embarrassed he was. Tucker and Basil rushed over to lap up the spilled liquid before it seeped into the cracks in the stone floor of the cave.

Stacy sighed and cupped his muzzle. "It's okay, Wink," she said, lifting him up. "Thank you for the milk. But you are never to go to the farm again, do you understand me?"

Addison had stepped into the cave just behind him, and Stacy realized she had to have a serious talk with her two mischief-makers.

"Listen, I appreciate how hard it must have been to drag this milk across the forest," Stacy said, picking up the bucket. There were a few drops left at the bottom and Stacy lifted the bucket to her lips and let them roll onto her tongue. "This deliciously creamy milk . . ." Stacy trailed off, temporarily forgetting why she was discouraging Wink from bringing her all-time favorite treat to her. Then she remembered the bounty. "And, Addison," Stacy continued sternly, "I know how quiet and careful you must have been when you nabbed the newspaper."

Addison and Wink both puffed up a bit at Stacy's praise.

"But what if the farmer had seen you, Wink? Or you, Addison, carrying a newspaper? I hate to break it to both of you but, from what I've read, neither of those things is normal behavior for a wolf. And anyway, I'd rather do without those luxuries than risk losing one of you. The last thing we need is a villager deciding they want to capture a 'magical' wolf, or worse, following you back to the forest with their gun."

Both wolves looked contrite—at least for the moment—but a sudden noise outside the cave startled all three of them.

I hope that's not a farmer looking for his milk bucket.

THREE

STACY AND THE wolves all breathed a sigh of relief when Everest and Noah sauntered into the cave. The noise hadn't been a farmer—just the sound of the two largest members of the pack returning from the morning's rescue.

Stacy shot Everest a look that said, *Let's talk later. Alone.* The massive wolf nodded. That was the thing about Stacy's wolves; she'd discovered that first fateful day in the forest that these particular wolves could understand her perfectly even though they lacked the ability to speak back. And they'd learned over the years to communicate with Stacy in other ways, either through facial expressions or body language. Stacy had gotten pretty good at reading them.

Might Everest already know about the problem with the other wolves? He had a kind of a sixth sense about the taiga and the animals that lived in it. He seemed to be able to read the mind of the forest. Stacy didn't know if Everest sensed something was wrong. Maybe he just wanted to scold her again for the morning's dangerous rescue mission. Either way, it would have to wait.

Stacy took the last bite of her sandwich and then stood up and brushed the crumbs from her jeans. She couldn't help smiling as Wink scarfed them up, his tail wagging back and forth with each nibble.

Stacy could see by the way the sunlight shone on the spruce trees outside the cave entrance that it was midafternoon. They had a couple hours of daylight left, and there was work to be done before they lost the light.

"Time for chores," she announced, grabbing her stone axe from beside the fireplace. "Addi, can you pull the lever, please?"

Addison trotted over to the Dog Decider, a rather rustic Rube Goldberg machine that she and Stacy had built together. What had started out as a self-assigned engineering homework project had turned out to be a remarkably useful tool for deciding which of the wolves got to help Stacy with the chores on a given day.

Addison took a wooden lever between her teeth and pulled. The lever knocked a small pinecone out of a wood cup and into an old bird's nest that sat on the apex of a wheel made of curved twigs that had been tightly woven together. The force of the pinecone turned the wheel, knocking the pinecone into a hollow tube made of birch bark that led to six others. Stacy pulled a second lever that caused the tubes to shift back and forth. She never knew which tube the pinecone would end up in, but that determined the winner—or perhaps the loser, depending on the chores Stacy had planned for that day.

The rock landed in front of one of six objects, each one representing a different wolf in Stacy's pack. Noah's object was a piece of blue beach glass he'd discovered during the pack's trip to the ocean biome that was to the east of them. Tucker's was a shiny copper penny, and Everest's a piece of strong, sturdy quartz. Addison was represented by a tiny pencil that had been sharpened past the point of being useful for writing, and Basil by a yellow dandelion Stacy had plucked from the forest and dried. Wink's object was a small red pocketknife he'd dug up near a campsite one day, its blade too rusty to use.

Stacy walked toward the cave entrance. Tucker stopped her on her way out. He had a scarf in his mouth.

"Thanks, Tuck," she said. "You're right, the late afternoons still get chilly." She wrapped the scarf around her neck and looked around the cave again. "Where did I leave my bag?"

Before she spotted it, Basil retrieved Stacy's satchel from a shelf in the back of the cave. She darted over to Stacy with it, Addison on her heels.

Stacy took her bag from Basil with one hand and held out the other for Addison, who dropped the red pocketknife into her palm.

"Thank you, Basil. Thank you, Addison," she said. "Wink, you're up."

Wink didn't budge. Normally all the wolves jumped at the chance to help Stacy with her chores. Except for Wink. Wink wasn't interested unless there was adventure involved. But today was a farming and woodcutting day, and Wink was apparently well aware of that fact.

"Wiiiinnnnkkkkk . . ."

Wink slowly started to stand, but Everest pushed past him and planted himself solidly by Stacy's side.

"Scratch that," Stacy said. "Wink, you've been spared. C'mon, Everest."

Wink excitedly spun around in place several times and plopped back down on the floor while Everest followed Stacy out of the cave. Stacy knew why Everest had volunteered: it would give her a chance to talk to him alone.

Stacy stepped into the forest and immediately took a deep breath of the pine- and spruce-scented air she'd come to love. She'd seen pictures in books and newspapers of countries and cities around the world. She'd seen photos of tropical islands and beaches and mountain biomes. But she couldn't imagine any biome more beautiful than their taiga forest.

Stacy and Everest started walking south of the cave through the forest. An ancient stream had formed their cave thousands of years ago. It was dug into the side of a steep ridge that towered over the tall pines and spruce trees that surrounded it. The ridge was the ideal vantage point from which to guard against any threats to Stacy and her wolves. Stacy also liked to climb up there to survey the world around her.

From the top, she could see that the taiga forest stretched as far south as any eye—human or wolf—could see. To the east was a deep ravine that separated the taiga from a giant oak forest. Entrances to an old abandoned iron mine could be found all along the ravine. That was a place Stacy generally avoided, always aware there could be a sudden cave-in. Even farther to the east, beyond the old oak forest, was the beach. That was the farthest Stacy and the wolves had ever traveled from their cave, and they'd only done it one time. It was the summer after Stacy had first read *Island of the Blue Dolphins* and she'd begged the wolves to show her the ocean.

To the west, on either side of the river, was a forest filled with towering birch trees. Even farther west, and a bit to the north, was a set of rolling hills that became low mountains. Directly north of the ridge was the swamp-lands, a patch of the forest that was permanently covered in a gray mist. A murky lake sat in the center of the swamp. On the rare occasions that Noah fished there instead of in the river, he always came back covered in slimy sludge and smelling of rotten plants. And lastly, even farther north, were tall, rugged mountains with snow-topped peaks year-round. The base of the extreme mountains was covered by a forest so dense it blocked out the sky to create a never-ending night. Stacy called that area the Forest of Perpetual Darkness. Stacy and her wolves had never had a reason to go there and her wolves had always balked at Stacy's desire to explore it in the past.

While she and Everest walked through the forest, she quietly told him what she had read in the newspaper.

"If we can persuade the other wolf pack to leave, I think the attention will die down," she said. "Do you think they'll go?"

Everest shook his head.

"Is there better hunting elsewhere?" Stacy asked. But she knew the answer was no. There were more than enough white-tailed deer, mule deer, and even moose to keep them satiated here in the taiga. *Come to think of it, why had they risked leaving and being shot by a farmer in the first place?*

"We should at least warn the other wolves about the bounty," Stacy continued. "Can't you explain it to them in wolf-speak? I'll come with you."

Everest shot her a look that said, *Yeah right.*

Sometimes Stacy forgot that not all wolves were as comfortable around humans as her pack was. It hadn't been until her first run-in with the wild pack that she learned wolves are naturally scared of humans and they most certainly do not understand English the way her wolf pack was somehow able to.

Stacy and Everest walked in silence for a little while. It wasn't an uncomfortable silence, though, it was the kind of quiet moment only two best friends could share. Each of them was completely at ease with the other and could allow their minds to wander while they walked.

Even though Stacy was pretty sure Everest never really allowed his mind to actually wander. That was the thing about Everest: he was always extremely present, keeping one step ahead of Stacy and looking out for danger.

Stacy's eyes began to well with tears. She knew she hadn't been entirely successful in explaining the seriousness of the wolf bounty to Everest. For as long as she could remember, she had always been afraid that *she'd* have to leave the wolves. She didn't know how she knew, but she believed that if humans discovered her, they'd force her to leave the life in the wild that she loved so much. It may have sounded strange to humans, but Stacy had no recollection of her family from before; *this* was her family and, as far as she was concerned, the only one that mattered. Which was why the idea of a wolf bounty going into effect and one of her wolves being taken from her . . . being killed . . . was a new fear on an entirely different level and Stacy couldn't bear the thought of it. She was relieved when she looked up and realized they'd arrived at their destination and she could focus on her chores.

Everest walked up to a cluster of tall spruce trees that grew so close together you could barely see between them and began pawing at the ground.

"Here, I'll help you, boy," Stacy said as she caught

up to him. She reached down and grabbed hold of a sheet of pine branches and dead roots that were bound together to create a crude trapdoor. Together they lifted the makeshift covering to reveal a wolf-size tunnel in the ground. Everest and Stacy wriggled through the short underground passageway that dipped a few feet beneath the cluster of thick trees and popped up on the other side in a small, sun-drenched clearing. There, in the protection of the giant spruce trees, was Stacy's small farm. It wasn't much, just a little patch of earth Stacy called a farm, with a few carrots, pumpkins, potatoes, and herbs she'd planted along with a hen, a rooster, and a half dozen or so baby chicks milling about. She reached into her satchel and pulled out a fistful of seeds, scattering them around. Fluff, the hen, and her little chicks eagerly pecked at them. The rooster, Crow, stood back as if he was too dignified to vie for food with his chicks, but then swept in to eat up when they appeared to be finished.

Next, Stacy took her metal canteen (left, months ago, hanging on a tree branch by a camper) out of her satchel and poured some water into a shallow bowl in the corner of the clearing. Everest lovingly nudged the baby chicks toward it.

Stacy didn't know how he could be so loving toward

something he would eventually eat. Stacy was more than happy to stick to her diet of fish, vegetables, berries, and the occasional treat Addison swiped from a campsite. But the wolves couldn't properly digest anything other than meat. They had given up hunting when they took Stacy in and, while Stacy could get them to eat some berries now and then when they were in season in the wild, she'd eventually had to start supplementing their diet with chicken. She knew wolves needed meat to survive. It was part of the circle of life. Hence, Fluff and Crow. She'd raised Fluff from when she was just a little yellow fluffball like the chicks scampering around her feet now. Stacy shuddered to think of the task ahead of her in a few months when the chicks were grown. She didn't like to dwell on that part, so she pushed the thought out of her mind. "Let's not name the chicks, okay?" she said, partly to herself. "It's bad enough I named Fluff and Crow."

After the chickens were fed, Everest used his paws to dig up a small bunch of carrots while Stacy used an old wooden hoe to uproot a potato. She filled her satchel with their small haul and then she and Everest exited the clearing via the dirt tunnel, making sure to close the branch door behind them.

On the way back to the cave, Stacy spotted a birch

sapling about the same height as her that had sprouted too close to a pine tree.

"That will never get enough sunlight to grow taller, Everest," she said. "Let's cut it up for kindling."

Stacy reached for her stone axe hanging on her satchel strap and went to work breaking down the sapling into small twigs.

As the sun was dipping below the tree line, she loaded the final stack of kindling into the pack that hung on Everest's back.

"Good job today, boy," Stacy said as they walked the rest of the way home. "Thanks for all your help." She thought back to the rabbit rescue earlier that day at the waterfall. Was that really just this morning? Stacy could tell Everest was still upset that he hadn't managed to stop her from jumping off the waterfall. Come to think of it, he'd been acting pretty sullen ever since. She'd have to make it up to him somehow. And she knew just the thing to improve his mood.

She dug into her satchel, searching below the potatoes and carrots for Everest's favorite toy—two old bones Stacy had found in the forest and lashed together with a piece of string. Stacy called it the throwbone.

"Hey, boy," Stacy said. "Want to play fetch?"

Everest's ears perked up at the sight of his toy. He

shook off his pack and took off running before Stacy had even raised her arm to throw. She hurled the bones as far as she could and a few seconds later Everest returned with it in his teeth, looking much happier than he had a few minutes before.

They got so caught up in their game that Stacy didn't notice the changes in the light until it was hard to see the throwbone flying through the air. The sun had completely vanished behind the trees.

"Hurry, Everest," she said. "We have to get back. The others will be howling for their dinner."

FOUR

AS SOON AS Stacy and Everest got back to the cave, she set about fixing the wolves' usual dinner—a sloppy but hearty chicken and pumpkin stew. Sometimes she threw in apples she'd scavenged, plus various herbs from her garden.

The wolves seemed to love Stacy's concoction, so, out of curiosity, she'd tried the stew herself once. It took an entire bucket of milk to wash the taste away. The wolves, however, didn't seem to mind the peculiar conglomeration one bit—in fact, they often wanted seconds.

Stacy ladled the stew into the six wooden bowls she had crafted for the pack last Christmas, each with a wolf's initial carved on the front. Their gift to her had been a leather journal, a pot of ink, and three quill pens that Addison had "found" in the village. Stacy didn't dare ask where exactly she'd found the items, but it was the perfect gift.

The wolves tucked into their dinner and Stacy walked over to the flat-topped boulder she and Noah had rolled into the cave last spring for Stacy to use as a desk. She sat on the tree stump in front of it, lit a candle, and opened the diary. She liked to record their animal rescues. She also jotted down one troubling note: *Possible wolf bounty. Not only will my wolves be vulnerable, there will be humans with rifles all over the forest. We'd have to go into hiding.*

She flipped to the back of the journal, where she kept track of the phases of the moon and the nightly wolf patrol rotation. Every night, one of the wolves paced along the ridge, guarding against any threats and keeping a lookout for animals in need of rescue.

"Full moon tonight, guys," she said loud enough to be heard over the dinnertime smacking and chomping. "And, Tucker, it's your turn to patrol the ridge."

As soon as she had finished her entry about the bunny, Stacy blew out the candle, grabbed her newspaper and pencil, and walked to the largest part of the cave near the opening. She hung a small pack over Tucker's hindquarters and gave him a quick kiss good-bye.

"There's some chicken jerky in there for when you get

hungry during the night," she said, ruffling the already messy tuft of fur on the top of his head. "Be safe, boy."

Tucker dipped his head in what could only be called a nod and trotted out into the forest, his tail wagging.

The sun and the moon set the pack's daily schedule in the forest. Darkness meant bedtime for everyone except the wolf on patrol. Stacy watched the others bed down for the night in what could only be called a puppy pile—a pile of very large puppies, anyway. She tiptoed into the center of the pile, newspaper in hand, taking extra care not to step on any tails.

She claimed a spot with her head on Everest's belly, her back to Noah's back, and her feet propped on Wink's backside.

Every night there was a slightly different sleeping arrangement, but to Stacy they were all equally comfortable. She was surrounded by creatures who loved her, who would lay down their lives for her. And she never needed a blanket. In the winter, she snuggled in tight so the wolves' thick fur would keep her warm. And in summer, the cool breezes in the forest wafted over them all.

Tonight was a special night because of the full moon—bright enough to shine through the cave opening so Stacy could work on the newspaper's crossword puzzle. Addison lay right behind her, her head on Stacy's

shoulder. Stacy propped a pair of drugstore reading glasses she'd found on Addison's snout so she could "help" with the answers.

"'Four across,'" Stacy read, "'type of Christmas tree. Six letters.'"

Addison's amber eyes were focused intently on the page. She didn't care much for news, but she loved crossword puzzles.

"A type of Christmas tree . . . Six letters . . . Not fir. Not pine. Spruce!"

Addison nudged her ear to let her know it was correct.

Stacy began to read the next clue, but she could hear Addison's breathing slow and deepen. A minute later, the wolf was snoring loudly in Stacy's ear. Stacy tucked the paper under her head, not wanting to complete too much of the puzzle without her best helper, and turned over, burying her head in Everest's soft fur. She drifted off, believing with all her heart that there was no better place to sleep in the world than nestled between five gigantic slumbering Arctic wolves.

Stacy fell into a deep sleep dominated by the dream she often had of her very first animal rescue. She had been with the wolves for just a month or two, running around the clearing playing tag with Wink and Addison, when she saw it—a baby owl. The owlet was so young it was just a little puff of fuzz and feathers.

"Where's your nest?" Stacy had asked, but of course it didn't answer her.

It was obvious that, without a mom, the poor creature would die. Stacy started crying while Wink and Addison hovered, wanting to help but not knowing how.

It was Tucker, Everest, and Noah who came to the rescue. Tucker began to lick the owlet like a mother bird while Everest scratched at the ground until he found some worms. Noah nudged a water bowl in the bird's direction.

After it had eaten, Basil curled herself around the bird to keep it warm.

For the next few weeks they lovingly took care of the owlet, which Stacy named Bramble. Soon, he grew the rest of his feathers and began to take short flights at night, but he always returned to the cave during the day.

Then, one night at dusk, Bramble soared into the air and Stacy saw that he was flying with other owls—one was a big adult and the others were just slightly larger than Bramble.

You found your family, Bramble. After that, they saw Bramble less and less. Stacy missed the little guy, but was happy for him.

That first rescue had awoken something inside of

Stacy. She knew what it was like to lose her own family. And how wonderful it was to be rescued (in her case, by the wolves). From then on, Stacy and the pack roamed the forest during the day, looking for ways to aid their fellow taiga residents. Reuniting families, saving animals from death, nursing the injured back to health . . . it became their work and their joy. She couldn't imagine a better life.

Stacy was just beginning to snore loudly when a bloodcurdling howl rang out over the quiet taiga. Stacy and the wolves all sat up at attention, every one of them wondering—and hoping—they'd dreamed it. But Stacy knew what she heard and it instantly filled her with dread. A second howl echoed through the trees. And it was definitely Tucker's.

FIVE

EVEREST, BASIL, NOAH, and Addison were out of the cave before Stacy had even wiped the drool from her face. They stopped for a brief moment outside to listen for the howl again and then disappeared from Stacy's sight.

Stacy turned to Wink, who was blinking his eyes in bewilderment, having been in a deep sleep. "Tucker's in trouble," Stacy said, quickly reaching for her boots.

Wink snapped to attention and lowered himself next to Stacy. "No, go without me!" Stacy said, tugging on her boots. "I'll be right behind you." There was no time for Stacy to tie her laces, even. She grabbed her satchel and ran out of the cave after Wink and into the night.

The howl had to have come from somewhere along the ridge. Wink set off up the hill after the rest of the pack with Stacy close on his heels. A thin switchback path led from the cave to the top of the ridge, but Stacy and the wolves had left it rough and hard to spot intentionally—always guarding against human discovery. Even with the full moon, Stacy couldn't see nearly as well as the wolves and was struggling to make it up the steep incline, her loose bootlaces flapping against her ankles.

Another howl pierced the air and Stacy stumbled over a branch.

Wink stopped and ran back to her, his eyes asking if she was all right.

"I'm fine, but I'm slowing you down," she said, tying her laces with fumbling fingers. "Go find the others. I'll catch up."

Wink lowered himself next to Stacy as if to say, *I'm not going anywhere without you,* and Stacy climbed on his back. When the trail got so steep it was almost a sheer climb, she could feel that Wink, despite his athleticism, was beginning to struggle.

"I can scale the rocks," Stacy said in his ear. "It'll be faster."

Wink crouched low to the ground and Stacy hopped off, bootlaces now tied tight. While Wink scrambled up the rest of the way, Stacy searched for hand- and footholds on the rocks. It was slow going, but she eventually found her footing and pulled herself up to a small ledge.

The ground was a little less steep after that and, with relief, she climbed onto Wink's back again. There was no time to lose.

Tucker's forlorn howl, closer now, confirmed that.

Finally, after what felt like forever but was probably closer to ten minutes, Stacy and Wink reached the top of the ridge. Stacy jumped off Wink and crouched down. She could see the paw prints of Everest, Basil, Noah, and Addison headed east. Stacy and Wink started running again, but only made it about twenty yards before they were both tackled to the ground by Basil.

"Basil! Why did you—" Stacy began to shout until Basil pressed her nose to Stacy's mouth, instantly quieting her. Everest ran up with a worried expression. Stacy and Wink exchanged a nervous glance and then followed Basil and Everest silently to where Addison and Noah were standing.

Stacy peered in the direction the other wolves were looking, through the thick trees and into a small clearing, and gasped in horror. There was Tucker, standing in the middle of the moonlit clearing surrounded by a pack of snarling wolves.

Stacy couldn't believe what her eyes were seeing. The wild pack had more than doubled in number since the last time she had seen them.

Eight, nine, ten . . . Stacy was counting the number of wolves from the pack. She had no idea they'd grown to this size. Everest motioned to some figures in the trees on the other side of the clearing. Stacy strained to make them out in the shadows.

"Eleven, twelve . . . wait, there are two pups, too?" Stacy queried urgently.

Everest nodded solemnly.

"Fourteen!" Stacy exclaimed quietly. "No wonder they're running out of food!"

Suddenly, Stacy noticed a small animal standing between Tucker's legs. It was a diminutive, snarling red fox. Tucker must have jumped into the middle of the pack to defend the creature.

But why? Stacy wondered. She hated the idea of the fox ending up as dinner for a wolf pack, but Tucker rarely showed any form of aggression. *The wolves are that desperate that they would eat a fox—a fellow member of the canine family?*

Stacy took a closer look.

"Whoa, that's a dog!" Stacy whispered. It did look remarkably like a fox, but it was definitely a dog. A dog with a gorgeous, fluffy tail and pointy ears.

Up until now, Stacy had never seen a dog in real life. She'd only seen pictures in books, but she'd always dreamed of someday having one as a pet. *How did a little dog manage to survive in the forest by itself?* And in that moment she knew that, like Tucker, she would do whatever she had to (including face down a pack of hungry wolves) to keep the little dog alive.

Everest emerged from the bushes with Stacy's other wolves following behind him. The two packs squared off on opposite sides of the clearing. Everest was almost nose-to-nose with the other pack's alpha. Stacy was surprised. The pack had a new leader, a female with a big bite taken out of her left ear—probably a battle wound from when she'd challenged the former alpha for lead position in the pack. She had obviously been successful. Stacy felt bad for the other wolf, who was likely now the pack's new beta.

Stacy remained in the bushes, studying the other wolves in the clearing. Almost all of them had black, gray, and brown fur, common for the type of wolves they were, except the alpha (who Stacy nicknamed Dusky in her head). She was beautiful. She was slender with long, lanky legs. Her fur was mostly gray, but also had patches of red and a cream underbelly. Each one of them looked underweight, particularly Dusky. Low growls rumbled in their throats while they waited to see what would happen. A signal from their alpha could lead to all-out war.

The wild wolves outnumbered Stacy's pack, but Everest and the others were stronger, smarter, and better fed.

Somehow, Everest was able to communicate that. The wild wolves knew they would lose any fight over the dog. With an almost imperceptible sign from Dusky, they backed down and, one by one, disappeared into the trees. As Dusky went to leave, she turned toward the bushes where Stacy was crouched and let out a low, nervous growl. Everest snarled a reply and, with that, Dusky slunk back into the shadows.

The dog had frozen in place for a moment as if it was stunned by its last-minute salvation, at the hands (or paws, rather) of wolves no less. Stacy strained her eyes to see if it was hurt. She knew basic first aid for animals from watching Tucker over the years. He was a remarkable healer and together they had brought injured animals to the cave for medical attention and rehabilitation.

Suddenly, the dog took off running.

"Let's go!" Stacy said to the others. *It could be hurt, or it could end up back in the middle of that wild wolf pack. Plus, I want a dog!*

The dog was fast, but so were they. They dashed after it, trying to be as silent as possible to avoid scaring it off. But six wolves and one girl dashing through the forest in the dark can't help but make a lot of noise.

There were downed trees to leap over, rocks to scale, hills to slide down. At one point Stacy climbed on Basil's back and she could hear the wind whistling in her ears as they scrambled down the steep ravine that separated their taiga from the old oak forest.

The dog knew the terrain. They lost it more than once and had to wait before Everest picked up its scent again. But he did pick it up.

Dawn was just beginning to break when Stacy spotted the tip of the fluffy red tail disappearing into a cave.

"There!" she shouted. "It ran into that cave!"

Everest tried to stop her from following the dog. This was a cave they'd never explored, which always meant possible danger. And there were unstable mine tunnels riddled throughout the area.

The other wolves seemed to be in agreement—all except Wink, who loved a good adventure.

"I'm going in," Stacy said forcefully. Wink was on her heels.

Reluctantly, the other wolves followed.

Stacy had learned to be ready for anything. From her satchel, she pulled out the materials to make a torch—a sturdy stick and a piece of an old T-shirt that she'd previously soaked with kerosene when a camper wasn't looking. She quickly wound the cloth around the stick and then used her knife to spark a piece of flint off the cave's wall. Seconds later, her torch was blazing.

The cave was dark and steep with none of the comforts Stacy and the wolves had brought into their own cave to make it homey. This cave was much longer than their own, with a sharp descent deep into the earth. Just when Stacy thought it would never end, the cave opened into the abandoned iron mine.

Stacy had always avoided this mine, which had a few entrances from the ravine. She didn't trust it not to collapse on top of her, but the dog might be injured and she was willing to risk her own safety to make sure the dog made it out alive.

She sensed Everest holding back, wanting to give up the rescue.

We have to try to help, Stacy thought, and she pushed

on, knowing the wolves wouldn't let her do so alone.

The torch revealed a mine cart on a rickety old railroad. Stacy hopped in and pumped the handle to get started, but soon the weight of the cart itself powered her farther and farther down into the mine while the wolves ran on either side of her.

They were moving deeper underground than Stacy had ever been before. The air was getting hotter and hotter. She knew Everest and the others were thinking they should give up and turn around. The dog clearly did not want to be rescued.

"That dog doesn't know we want to help it," Stacy yelled. Her words echoed off the smooth stone walls. "It'll die down here if we don't get to it."

Water dripped from the walls. They kept running into swarms of bats, and Stacy felt like her face had been cocooned by broken cobwebs. But they pressed on. They kept going until they reached the very end of the mine cart's track.

The mine had become a rugged cave again. Stalagmites jutted up from the floor while stalactites hung from the ceiling. They wove in and out of them, and then came to what could only be described as a cave within the cave—a hole going down, down, down.

The descent was too steep for them to navigate

without help. After a quick consultation with Addison, Stacy reached for the long, thick rope in Tucker's pack—rope they had woven themselves from sturdy vines. She threaded it around the mine cart's wheel and used a bowline knot to attach it to the mine cart's lever. Then she wrapped the other end around Everest.

The cart would serve as a sort of pulley so they could lower themselves through the deep hole. They'd be able to use it to help get them back up again, too.

Everest went first.

I hope the rope is long enough, or I don't know what we'll do.

Finally, Everest signaled to Stacy with a tug on the rope. He had reached the bottom. He slipped out of his pack and they raised it up again.

Stacy was the next to go down, followed by Addison, Wink, and Noah. Basil and Tucker would stay with the mine cart in case anything went wrong and they needed additional help.

As soon as everyone reached the bottom, Stacy gave two quick tugs on the vine to make sure that Basil and Tucker were aware they had made it down safely. Then they all untied themselves and set off after the dog again.

The cave became hotter and hotter the deeper they went. Stacy raised her torch to reveal steamy pools of water and magma, the molten rock found beneath the earth's crust, around them.

"Be careful," Stacy said. "We're deep, deep in the earth. If you miss a step, you'll—"

The word *die* got stuck in Stacy's throat when she spotted the dog. It was standing in the center of a very small rock, surrounded by magma. One wrong move and it would be burned to death.

SIX

THE DOG WAS perched on a small rock in the middle of the magma, like a queen in her castle surrounded by a moat. The dog must have jumped out onto the rock when it was running down the cave at full speed. Now it didn't have the momentum to make the jump back. One clumsy move would mean certain death for the dog.

The dog eyed them, now more frightened by what was happening around it than by the wolves.

"Don't worry, little one, we'll find a way to rescue you," Stacy said. The confidence in her tone didn't match what she was really feeling. She took a deep breath and tried not to let panic overwhelm her. The intense heat seared her lungs and made sweat pour down every inch of her body, stinging her eyes and dripping onto the hot rocky floor below her with an angry hiss.

Everest stood slightly in front of Stacy making sure she didn't get too close to the magma, while Wink had his teeth on Stacy's satchel, holding her back. Addison paced behind her, her tongue lolling, panting to release some of her body heat. Stacy could practically hear the gears in her mind turning, trying to figure out a way to rescue the dog. And Noah, poor, river-diving Noah, had never been more out of his element.

All the wolves paced around nervously, waiting for Stacy's direction. Whatever they were going to do, they had better do it quickly.

Stacy looked around, searching for anything that would help them rescue the little dog.

Wink was the biggest daredevil of the group, and Stacy was sure he was gauging if he could make the jump over and back with the dog, but one wrong move and they would lose both him and the dog.

"No," Stacy said, assessing the distance. "The small rock will teeter and both you and the dog will fall into the magma. No leaping. But maybe we can build a bridge of some kind."

Everest was getting restless. He put his teeth on the

back of Stacy's shirt and gave a small tug, pulling her backward.

She kneeled down and took his face in her hands, whispering so that the little dog wouldn't hear. "I know it looks hopeless," she said. "But let's think. I'm not ready to give up."

Everest growled a warning. Over his head, Stacy saw the dog begin to turn around and tremble, making the rock wobble even more.

"It's okay," Stacy cooed. "Try not to move too much."

As she said that, even more magma bubbled up. The distance between them and the dog grew. Stacy raised her torch and studied the wall behind the dog—the magma moat was narrower behind the dog, and the wall had what looked like a ledge. But it was too small for Stacy's feet. And that was assuming Stacy could make the jump in the first place, which she wasn't confident about.

"Is there anything we can use to build a bridge?" Stacy asked. She tried to remember some of the lessons she and Addison had skimmed in a *Physics for Idiots* book they had uncovered in the library's recycling bin. Stacy had originally been insulted by the title, but the book proved to be incredibly useful at teaching basic physics. The problem was, none of the tools or equipment the book suggested were available deep down in the cave.

She tore a strip of fabric off the bottom of her shirt and tied her hair in a ponytail with it, trying to stop the streams of sweat from falling into her eyes. She raised the torch again and examined the walls and floors, searching for a loose piece of anything that might serve as a bridge.

The wolves had picked up on Everest's uneasiness. Stacy could feel it. But their loyalty to her overwhelmed whatever else they were thinking. They set out in search of materials.

A few minutes later, Stacy heard a noise behind her and turned to see that Noah and Wink were both pushing a thin sheet of shale toward her. The chunk of rock looked as if it had been sheared off the cave walls, maybe in a rockslide. The shale fragment was too short to form a bridge that would stretch across the moat, but at least it was something.

"Great job, guys," Stacy said. "I think we can work with this."

Everest growled again—at Noah and Wink for searching for tools and at Stacy for even considering such a dangerous rescue.

"I know I can't get onto the dog's rock island," Stacy assured him. "But using it as a plank I might be able to get close enough to grab it."

Everest shook his head, but he knew there was no talking her out of trying. He paced nervously while Stacy searched through her satchel for her leather gloves. They would help her hold on to the shale. One slip of a sweaty palm would send her careening into the magma.

At least it would be a fast death. And I'd die doing what I loved—rescuing an animal—surrounded by my wolf family.

It was as if Everest could read her thoughts. He stopped short and gave her a warning growl. *Don't do this,* his facial expression said. *Just don't.*

"I have to try," Stacy whispered to Everest. "And if I slip, don't get any ideas about being a hero. The pack can't lose both of us."

She could almost hear Everest scoff, but she hoped her words got through. She didn't want him jumping in after her. Then she began speaking softly to the dog again. "It's okay. It's okay. We're friends."

Noah and Wink helped her tug the long piece of shale over to the moat. It was hard to believe it could get any hotter, but the nearer they got to the magma, the higher the temperature rose.

They carefully extended the slab halfway over the edge. Just as Stacy had feared, it was short by a couple of feet. If they let go, it would fall and be lost. But . . . if she could find something to place underneath the sheet of shale at its center, it could work like a kind of seesaw to give her the height she needed to make the jump. It just needed a fulcrum. Stacy looked around the cave. There were several small boulders that might work, but all of them would likely make the seesaw too dangerous. If the boulder were to roll out from under the slab, Stacy would be done for. No, that wouldn't work.

The sound of metal scraping against the cave floor echoed through the chamber and Stacy turned around to see Addison. She was back from her supply scouting mission and dragging a rusty old pickaxe behind her.

"Perfect, Addi," Stacy said, lifting the heavy pickaxe. "Stand back, everyone. I've got an idea."

Stacy struggled to lift the pickaxe to her shoulders. It was so much heavier than she expected it would be. Using all her strength, she brought the pickaxe up over her head and let gravity do the rest, smashing the pickaxe down on the cave floor and taking out a sizable chunk of bedrock.

"If I can chip away enough of an area, leaving a small strip of raised rock at the edge, we can make a shale seesaw!"

Stacy had never seen a wolf roll its eyes before, but that's exactly what Everest was doing. Meanwhile,

Addison was nodding her head slowly, as if she was still working out in her mind whether Stacy's plan was sound. Noah and Wink mostly just looked confused. Stacy understood where Everest was coming from. It was really, really risky. Shale was not the sturdiest of sedimentary rocks. Essentially hardened mud made up of bits of clay, quartz, and calcite, it could easily break apart at any moment without warning, sending Stacy to a fiery grave. This was a particularly thick slab, though, and Stacy liked her chances.

"Everest, please," Stacy pleaded. "This dog is running out of time and options. I believe this will work."

Stacy carried on swinging the pickaxe, breaking up more of the bedrock with each hit. After a few minutes, she'd managed to clear a couple of feet. Stacy was exhausted. She sat down and took a sip from her canteen while the wolves all worked to clear the tiny pieces of rubble from where she'd been mining.

With all the small rocks out of the way, Everest helped Stacy drag the slab over the edge once more. Only now, instead of dangling precariously over the edge, the shale lay at an incline in the groove Stacy had pickaxed. The other end—the one that hovered over the magma—rose like a seesaw.

Stacy stood on the end of the slab and indicated for

Everest and Addison to join her, which they did.

"All right, here goes nothing," Stacy whispered.

With Everest and Addison standing on the end, Stacy began to slowly walk up the plank on her hands and knees. Just as she had hoped, the shale held steady with the weight of the wolves on the other side. Stacy reached the top and peered over the edge, a decision she immediately regretted. She centered her weight on the slab and took a deep breath.

"Okay, Addison," she said calmly, "listen closely. I want you to step your back legs off the slab."

Stacy braced herself for what she knew was coming. Addison let out a series of short, piercing barks that echoed loudly off the cave walls. A clear objection to Stacy's plan. She didn't even want to know what Everest's expression was and she didn't dare risk moving to turn her head around to see.

Suddenly, Stacy lurched forward on the slab, sliding a couple of inches toward the edge. Addison, surprisingly, had done what Stacy had told her to and stepped one leg off the slab, but now Stacy was closer to the magma than ever before. The dog let out a painful yelp. Stacy could now see that it had a small burn on one of its front paws.

"Okay, good Addi," Stacy breathed out. "Now the other back leg, slowly."

Addison stepped off the slab with her other hind leg, making sure to keep both her front paws firmly planted on the slab with Everest. Stacy was lowered a few more inches and the dog was just barely out of reach now. The poor thing cowered even more, whimpering in fear and pain.

Stacy reached around behind her back and grabbed a small rope out of her satchel. She tied it around her waist and threw the other end to Noah and Wink. "Hold on to the rope. I might need your help to balance on my way back."

They stood one behind the other, grasping the rope in their teeth. Stacy could see that they didn't understand how this would help—neither did she, really—but she wanted to give them a job to do. It seemed a sensible thing at the moment.

She almost laughed at herself. *If I was sensible. I'd still be asleep in the cave. At least with the rope they'll have my bones to bury if I fall in. Or does magma melt bones . . . ?*

She shook the thought off and began to inch her way over the edge of the shale.

"I love you guys," she said over her shoulder.

She heard Wink whimper behind her.

Stacy was as far as she could go at the end of the slab. She extended her arm toward the little dog, who was

now just inches away from her grasp.

"Here, little one," she said. "Be a good dog and come to me."

Stacy expected the little dog to whimper, or even growl. But instead she heard a sound that sent shivers down her spine and made the hairs on the back of her neck stand up in fear.

"Oh no," Stacy groaned.

The shale had begun to crack.

SEVEN

STACY CLOSED HER eyes and took a shallow breath. She almost didn't dare breathe at all. Slowly, she turned her head back around to the wolves to see if they'd also spotted the growing crack in the shale slab. Everest had. He was staring intensely at it, almost willing the crack to not spread any more than it already had. Addison's, Wink's, and Noah's eyes were all trained on Stacy. All the while she crooned a lullaby to keep the little dog, and the wolves, calm:

> *Hush, little doggy, don't howl or moan.*
> *Stacy's gonna bring you a nice big bone.*

And if that bone's gone when you wake,
Stacy's gonna bring you a juicy steak.
And if Wink steals that steak from you,
Stacy's gonna bring—

Stacy had always wondered where she had learned the original version of that song. It was as if she had always known it. She had been making up her own words to the melody for so long that she didn't even remember how the song was supposed to be sung. Now wasn't the time for memories anyway. She shook it off and replaced it with determination.

I can do this, she thought.

Stacy took one more shallow breath in and leaned forward, now completely reliant on the rope that Wink and Noah were still holding on to. She began to reach her arm out toward the dog. Only, she didn't have to. Suddenly, and quite unexpectedly, the dog leapt onto Stacy's head and then leapt again onto the shale behind her, causing the crack to double in size and spread quickly up toward Stacy. The dog scurried off the slab and past Everest and Addison to safety.

"That works, too," Stacy grumbled matter-of-factly, spinning around quickly and jumping toward the wolves as the shale cracked in half and fell into the magma, sizzling as it sunk.

Stacy fell to her knees and gave all the wolves big hugs, beginning with Everest. His eyes were stern, but Stacy knew that was because he loved her. Addison gave her big, slurpy kisses and Wink and Noah nuzzled her cheeks.

Stacy scooped up the little dog that had caused so much trouble. It eyed them all curiously. It didn't seem to be afraid of them any longer, but Stacy didn't trust it not to run. After all they risked saving it, she needed to make sure it was unhurt.

She ran her hands up and down its body and then its legs. There were no visible cuts or obvious broken bones. There was a small burn on her foot—yes, it was a girl—which Noah was already treating with tender licks. But other than that, the dog seemed fine. And she was accepting Noah's attention with a calm poise.

"I guess you've decided wolves are okay after all," Stacy said, giving her a good scratch. "Now let's go home. You need to rest. We all do."

The walk back to the hole that led up to the mine seemed a lot longer on the way back. Everyone was exhausted by the heat and the effort they had made.

Stacy had drunk all the water in her canteen, so the wolves and the dog licked at the water droplets that ran down the cave walls as their elevation got higher. Stacy welcomed air that had seemed scorching on the way down, but now felt cool compared to the blistering heat generated by the magma.

"Maybe we should find a way to plug that hole when we get back up there," Stacy said as they neared the deep chasm that had led them from the mine to the dog. "That way, no other animals will find themselves in the same position as this little pooch here."

Everyone—including the pooch—shot her a double take. There were no words required for Stacy to know what *that* meant.

"Okay, okay," she answered. "We'll come back another day. We're too exhausted to do a good job now anyway."

Stacy gave Everest's head a quick pat. He would suffer more than any of the others if something were to happen to her. The other wolves had him to turn to and rely on, but Everest and Stacy relied on each other.

A minute later they reached the bottom of the deep hole and Stacy was shouting up to Tucker and Basil, who howled with relief when they heard Stacy's voice and Everest's low rumble.

"You're up first, Noah," Stacy said, tying the dangling rope around him. Then she shouted up to Basil, who used the cart's lever to reverse the pulley system. Once Noah had reached the top, they dropped the rope again.

Addison went next and then Wink. Everest insisted on being raised last, so Stacy, with the dog in her arms, was lifted next.

There was another joyful reunion when Everest finally made it to the top and they were all together again.

"And this is our dog," Stacy said. "She doesn't have a name yet, but she's coming home with us—at least for now." She put her own nose up against the dog's. "For as long as she wants."

The dog seemed to understand. She wagged her tail and jumped into the mine cart with Stacy. The torch had long since burned out, but they had the track to follow. Stacy pumped the lever to get them started. Going uphill was harder than going down, so Tucker and Basil got behind and pushed—the others were too exhausted. With each foot they rose, the air got clearer and cooler. It wasn't long before Stacy was shivering. She couldn't wait to bed down among her wolves, warmed by their thick fur.

But bed was a long way off. It took quite a bit of time

to reach the entrance to the old iron mine, and then there was the deep ravine to climb up before they made their way to the taiga.

Now that the danger was over, Stacy became aware of every scrape and bump she'd earned on their climb up the ridge and their race down the cave. Her eyes were red and sore from all the salty sweat. And her arms were exhausted with the effort of holding the sleeping dog.

They all needed baths in clean, cool water and they needed to take care of their wounds. And most of all they needed sleep.

They got closer to their part of the taiga. The sky changed from black to purple to gray as the sun began to rise. Even with the light, Stacy stumbled a couple times before Basil lowered herself by Stacy's side to invite her to climb on, dog in arms.

Stacy did so, and buried her face in Basil's fur, smelling the scorching sulfur stench that had permeated every inch of them when they were deep in the cave.

They reached the mouth of their cave and Stacy tumbled off Basil onto the floor—too tired to even try to stand. She laid the dog down and simply sat with her head against the wall, trying to keep her eyes open. There were things she needed to do.

Noah pushed a water bucket in Stacy's direction and

she drank until her stomach couldn't hold any more. Then, without cleaning her wounds, without making sure that everyone was taken care of, or even that the dog was really settled, Stacy allowed Tucker and Everest to lead her to their sleeping area. She was only vaguely aware of the wolves quietly padding around her as she dropped off to sleep.

EIGHT

STACY'S DREAMS WERE fueled by the intense heat from the cave and by the real lyrics to that lullaby, which she seemed to have dug up from her memory. Mockingbirds flitted about with wings made of diamonds while billy goats and dogs chased each other through fiery castles.

Every once in a while she became aware of wolves moving around her. At one point, she could feel Tucker licking and cleaning her scratches while another wolf, Noah probably, washed her blistered skin with cool water from the river. Too tired even to say thank you, Stacy drifted off again.

Later, she tried to open her eyes when Everest pushed a piece of bread toward her lips. Only then did she realize she was ravenous. She chewed slowly, too tired to move. After she had swallowed a few bites, Everest seemed to be satisfied. He lay down next to her again and Stacy blocked out the bright sunshine at the cave's entrance by burying her face in his thick fur.

She briefly wondered how the wolves could to do anything at all besides sleep, but they had always had deeper energy reserves than she did. She drifted off again.

After some time had passed, Stacy slowly became aware of the sounds around her—birdsong reached her from outside the cave's entrance, and there was the quiet, steady breathing of her protector. Without even opening her eyes, she knew it was Everest keeping watch over her. She dragged herself up to a seated position and looked around. The sun was just beginning to set.

The other wolves were out and about, but Everest stood guard next to her.

"Is the dog still here?" she asked. "She didn't run away, did she?"

Everest nodded, but Stacy realized she didn't know which question he was answering yes to.

"She's still here?" Stacy asked again, hopeful.

The alpha wolf nodded once more, and somehow Stacy knew he wouldn't have let the dog leave—at least not until she had taken a good look at her.

"I'm so glad." Stacy rubbed her face again. Her brain felt like it was filled with cobwebs. "I guess I slept all day," she said to him.

He cocked his head with a questioning look.

"Two days?" Stacy asked incredulously.

Everest nodded. Stacy took a deep breath and began to move her arms and legs. "I'm fine," she said. "A little stiff is all. Okay, a lot stiff." She checked out her scratches, which were already healing. A deep purple bruise on her shin was tender to the touch, but her skin, which had felt like it had been scorched by the earth's heat when she fell asleep, was cool. Tucker truly was an expert healer.

Everest nudged the water bucket in her direction and Stacy lifted it for a good, long drink. And then she ate the rest of the bread. Everest waited patiently for her to finish before trotting toward the back of the cave. When he returned, the little dog was with him.

Her reddish-brown, bushy tail wagging like crazy, the dog jumped into Stacy's lap and started licking her face. Before long Stacy was giggling.

"All right, settle down, you crazy girl," Stacy said, giving the dog a good scratch.

It took a few minutes, but the dog settled in her lap, her head on Stacy's knee. She eyed the cave's opening with a curious expression as if to say, *What's next?*

Too tired to do anything else, Stacy grabbed a book from the shelf above her head and started turning the pages. She settled into one of her favorite chapters, enjoying the feeling of being home, being safe, and having a dog in her lap—the wolves were much too big for that.

Stacy already knew this dog was fearless, having stood her ground against the wild wolf pack and jumping over the magma to safety. It turned out she was also quite smart, using her nose to help her turn the pages of the book at exactly the right intervals.

Before Stacy could explore the dog's talents further, Wink and Noah backed into the cave. Wink was dragging a bucket of Stacy's stew while Noah was dragging a water bucket. Addison, Basil, and Tucker weren't far behind.

There was a little celebration when they all saw that Stacy was awake and unhurt, and she took a moment to greet and thank each wolf for their help with the rescue and for taking such good care of her and the dog.

Then she dished out the stew in the six bowls, saving some for the little dog. She checked for a spare food bowl and settled on the broken plastic canteen a camper had carelessly thrown into the woods after it split in two, forming two receptacles.

Humans. Stacy almost growled when she thought the word. But the campers' careless disdain for the forest did come in handy time and time again.

The makeshift bowl was the perfect size for a small dog dish. Stacy filled it with the stew and set it down in the same row as the wolves' bowls.

"C'mere, girl," Stacy said. "Dinnertime."

The dog understood. She ran right over.

Stacy kneeled next to her to watch her eat. She didn't know what the dog was used to eating, but she slurped up her pumpkin chicken stew in two or three bites. It made Stacy happy to see the dog fitting right in and doing so well.

"You can stick around for as long as you want," Stacy told her, scratching behind her ears. "But you'll need a name, won't you?"

The dog looked up at Stacy and wagged her red-tinted tail.

"Scarlett?" Stacy said, trying it out.

The dog looked unimpressed.

"You're right. Too dainty." Stacy eyed the book she had set aside to serve dinner. "I know! We'll call you Page, like a page in a book."

Page seemed to approve. She jumped up and put her front legs on Stacy's knee.

"Can you . . . understand me?" Stacy asked in disbelief. She leaned over to pet the dog, and was met with a big, sloppy kiss in return.

"Page it is, then," she said. She introduced her to each of the wolves by name. One by one they pressed their noses against the dog's to say hello and welcome.

"I guess you're a member of the pack now," Stacy said. "But stay away from those other wolves—the wild ones. Until we find them a better food source."

Stacy was about to tell the dog more, but all of a sudden a bat flew past her head. Its wings almost brushed against her hair. She jumped. Then she noticed a few more bats hanging from the shelves at the back of the cave. That was unusual. She had worked hard filling the holes in the cave walls with mud to try to make it a place that bats didn't want to inhabit. She believed that all living creatures had a right to live in the forest—except the humans who wanted to hunt or build or destroy— but bats had a habit of startling her. They came out of nowhere and disappeared just as quickly. Stacy would never say she hated any animal that called the taiga home, but secretly she did hate bats. A lot.

That's weird. . . and annoying, she thought. *At least they'll all be outside for the night soon.*

She turned away, not noticing that Page's ears swiveled each time one flew by.

NINE

AFTER THE WOLVES had finished their dinner, Stacy cleaned and put away their bowls and turned to face the reposing pack.

"Okay," she announced, rubbing her hands together, "I know we've had a long couple of days. Is there anyone who isn't rested enough for chores or guard duty?"

Wink walked over and put his head on her knee with the saddest expression he could muster. Stacy burst out laughing. She knew that if anyone had been sleeping all day, it was him.

Everest let out an affectionate growl. He often let Wink off the hook when it came to guard duty. But tonight neither one of them was on call. Stacy checked her diary.

"Basil, you're up," she said. "Can you handle it?"

Basil came over and rubbed Stacy's nose with hers.

"Thanks, girl," Stacy said, scratching the she wolf's back. "We'll see you in the morning."

Basil dashed out of the cave. A couple of bats followed her.

"What's up with the bats, Everest?" Stacy asked.

If a wolf were capable of shrugging, Everest would have. He clearly wasn't bothered by them.

"At least they eat mosquitoes," Stacy muttered to herself. She walked over to the Dog Decider and pulled the lever. Page watched with interest as the river rock dropped out of its wooden cup and into the bird's nest on the top of the wheel before finding its way into the birch bark tube.

Finally, it landed in front of the pencil.

"Addison, it's your turn," Stacy said. "It's too dark to do much. We're just going to feed the chickens tonight. The farm can wait until tomorrow."

Addison grabbed Stacy's satchel with her teeth and brought it to her. They set out for the chicken coop with Page on their heels. Stacy was relieved to see that someone, probably Noah, had already filled the water buckets. She wasn't looking forward to a walk to the spring.

Before she had even lifted the branch trapdoor at the coop, Stacy knew something was wrong. It was too quiet.

Her heart sank when she came through the tunnel into the clearing and her suspicions were confirmed. There were feathers everywhere. But not a single chick in sight. Crow and Fluff were missing as well.

Eaten by the wild wolves, Stacy surmised. Her shoulders slumped and tears immediately formed in her eyes.

Addison nuzzled Stacy's hand, while Page looked on confused and began playing with the feathers. Of course the dog didn't know their flock was missing, or why.

"They were doing what they need to do to survive," Stacy said, her voice quivering. "To feed their pups."

And then she saw it: perched high up in one of the spruce trees was Fluff. Poor Fluff. She must have flown up there hoping her chicks would be able to follow. Stacy looked up at Fluff and then down at the trunk of the spruce. There in the small space between the towering trees was a pair of gold eyes staring back at her. Dusky. Stacy let out a loud gasp, which, in turn, scared Dusky off. Addison and Page came over to the base of the tree and Stacy used Addison's back as a stepping stool to reach Fluff and bring her down. Together they all walked back to the cave in silence.

I've lost my main food source for my wolves. Stacy kicked the dirt and wiped a tear from her cheek. She couldn't believe how careless she'd been. She knew the wild wolves were expanding their hunting trips. Why hadn't she thought to have one of her wolves guard the chickens? Everest was going to be mad at himself for not thinking of it either.

Noah must have caught a trout earlier that day. He had wrapped it in leaves and set it on a small rock ledge that jutted out over the fire. The smell tickled Stacy's nostrils the minute she reentered the cave.

"Thanks, Noah," Stacy said. "I'm starving."

She used a wide, flat stick to lift the fish off the ledge and onto the piece of shale she used for a plate. Even though she'd eaten earlier, Page eyed her with the sweetest of looks and Stacy couldn't help but laugh.

"Okay," she said. "I'll share. It's a reward for the fact that you haven't tried to eat Fluff yet." Stacy glanced up at Fluff, who had roosted high up on the bookcase.

When Stacy had finished her meal, she set the fish bones aside. One of her gardening books said animal bone meal was an excellent fertilizer and that had turned out to be true. But she didn't have the heart to go back to the farm tonight. It was too sad.

"Don't eat those," she warned Page. "They'll get stuck in your throat."

Stacy headed out to the clearing in front of the cave with Everest, finding her way by starlight. Stacy hated to ruin the beautiful night with her terrible news. Reluctantly, she told the alpha wolf about the chicken massacre.

"I mean, should we have Noah fish more so we can bring food to the wolves and they won't have to go to the farms?" Stacy wondered aloud as she began to pace outside the cave with Everest. "That's only a temporary solution, though. They've outgrown this part of the taiga. Some of them need to move deeper into the forest;

they need to start a new pack. But how can we convince them to do that? They're a family unit. . . . It would be like someone telling our pack to separate. We'd never do it."

Everest stared at the ground, his icy-gray eyes expressing concern.

"It's going to be all right, boy," Stacy said, gently patting Everest on his head. "We'll figure this out, just like we figure out all our other animal rescues."

But deep down, Stacy was worried. This wasn't like any of their previous rescues. Trying to force a large pack of wolves to move territories was nothing like saving a rabbit from drowning or feeding a baby owl. In fact, these wolves didn't even know they were in danger at all.

"These wolves are members of our taiga family, same as any other creature," Stacy said to Everest, his head raising to meet her gaze. "We have to find a way to protect them . . . somehow."

TEN

OVER THE NEXT few weeks, Stacy was constantly on alert for the sound of bullets. It wasn't hunting season yet, so if shots rang out, it would mean that the wolf bounty law had been passed. Each night she went to sleep relieved that there hadn't been any gunfire.

Page, in the meantime, became an integral part of the pack. She swam in the river with Noah, played with Wink and Addison, tagged along with Tucker when it was his turn to patrol the ridge, and obeyed Everest and Basil on the rare instances she got too rambunctious.

"I think she believes she's a wolf," Stacy said to Everest one day while they were digging for potatoes at the farm. "It's hard to believe she ran from us that first night." Stacy sat back on her heels and watched Page. The dog was just outside the spruce grove, playing tag with a rabbit. The rabbit was not amused by Page's game in the least.

"She's not a hunter, that's for sure. She'll fit right in on our rescue missions."

Everest seemed to agree, but he stopped digging for a moment when a bat zoomed past.

Page stopped what she was doing and it looked like her ears twitched in the bat's direction, but then she started to play with the rabbit again and Stacy decided she must have imagined it.

It's strange how bats have been showing up a lot more since Page joined us. Stacy thought about it the whole walk home to the cave.

A few mornings later, Page started barking and wouldn't stop. She jumped up and down in front of Stacy, running a few feet away and then circling back.

"You want us to go somewhere, don't you, Page?" Stacy asked.

The dog yipped something that sounded remarkably like *finally* and took off. A couple of bats zoomed in front of her.

Page must have startled them from their roosts, Stacy thought. But there wasn't time to worry about the bats. Page needed Stacy and the wolves for something.

"Come with me, Everest. Basil and Tucker, you, too," Stacy said, taking off after the dog. "Everyone else stay close in case we need you."

They raced through the taiga. It was just after dawn and Stacy was still a little groggy. Page didn't even look over her shoulder, trusting the wolves would follow. Stacy struggled to keep her eyes on the dog's red tail, leaping over roots and rocks and puddles from the previous night's rain to stay with her.

After a mile or so, Page suddenly stopped, and Stacy saw what the problem was.

An adult doe had been shot with a bow and arrow and was lying on the forest floor, motionless. Stacy immediately kneeled down. If there were humans around, she definitely didn't want to be seen. The wolves paced, as on edge as she was. Humans could be unpredictable and dangerous at the best of times, and these particular humans were hunting outside of the official archery season. Obviously they didn't care about rules.

Everest and Basil took a few steps out in opposite directions of Stacy, creating a defensive perimeter. Tucker was at the doe's side, assessing her wounds. Stacy lowered herself and pressed her ear to the mossy earth. She listened carefully, but heard nothing that sounded like humans.

"Tucker, is she . . ." Stacy trailed off as she glanced up to meet Tucker's gaze. His head hung low, his coppery eyes glinted in the sunlight, as if he might cry. The doe was dead. Stacy knew wolves didn't cry from emotion like humans did, but she also knew that Tucker was an exceptionally sensitive wolf. Her heart ached for him. She knew how much Tuck hated losing an animal of the forest.

The fact that the humans responsible weren't even around made the doe's death all the more infuriating. Stacy knew some humans hunted for food, just like many of the animals in the forest. But if no one was looking for this doe, then they had killed her merely for sport. Stacy put her hand on Tucker's side to show her support as he gently pulled the arrow from the doe's chest and offered it to her.

She grabbed hold of the arrow and snapped it in half over her knee. If the humans did stumble upon their kill, she'd at least make sure they couldn't use this particular arrow again. She covered the wound with some wildflowers. It was the only thing she could do for the doe.

She was about to suggest that they look around to make sure the doe didn't have a fawn with her when she saw something moving out of the corner of her eye.

Dusky was stalking slowly toward Stacy. Her gold eyes glittered with hunger. Three of her largest wolves were behind her. Stacy saw several more wolves behind them in the trees.

Everest bristled and stood his ground. But it wasn't Stacy they were after.

"They want the doe," Stacy whispered. "They can have it. And anyway, we need to look for a fawn. It's early enough in the day that it would probably still be nearby if she had one."

Suddenly, Stacy realized Page was not with them. A wave of dread rushed over her. Page looked so much like a fox, and hunters would not hesitate to shoot a fox. Stacy put the terrible thought out of her head and sprang to her feet.

"Basil!" Stacy whispered as loud as she could. "Find Page, as fast as you can. Tucker, stand guard while the wolves feed. Make sure the hunters aren't coming for the deer." Basil started running before Stacy had even finished her sentence. Stacy turned her head toward Everest, who gave a knowing nod back to her. Immediately, she began racing in the same direction as Basil, with Everest on her heels. Stacy pumped her arms as she sprinted through the trees, knowing she'd have to push herself to keep up with Basil. Behind her, Tucker was unable to contain his emotions any longer. He raised his head and let out a heart-wrenching howl that echoed all through the taiga. He gave the doe one last sorrowful look as the wild wolves made quick work of its body.

They found Page waiting patiently for them next to a fawn, tucked away in a bed of ferns. A bat fluttered around the two of them.

The first time Stacy had stumbled across a newborn fawn in the forest, she had been convinced its mother had abandoned it. The wolves knew better, though, and Stacy soon learned that mother deer often hid their fawns in order to protect them while they scavenged for food.

Fawns are born with no scent—nothing a potential predator on the hunt could pick up. They are also unsteady on their feet, unable to run if a predator picks up on their mother's scent and comes after them. Which is why mothers leave their young, returning to feed them until the fawns are strong enough to join them.

But this poor fawn's mother would never return. Stacy and the wolves couldn't raise it. It needed a mother's milk to survive. They'd have to find another doe and hope it was willing to nurse the little thing.

Basil lowered herself next to the fawn. Constellations of white spots covered its golden-brown back and legs. Its eyes were barely open. There was no time to lose to get it to safety, especially with the wild wolves around. The fawn was so small, so new. Stacy could feel its heart pulsing as she picked it up and carefully lowered it over Basil's back.

"Good job, Page," Stacy said. "Now we need to find a mama deer to take in this little one."

Once again, Stacy had the distinct impression that Page understood. Her ears swiveled back and forth like she was searching for some sound. Then she trotted off, leading them to a clearing a few hundred yards away where, sure enough, a few deer were grazing, including a doe and her fawn.

"Here, Basil," Stacy said, carefully scooping the fawn from her back. "I have a feeling the deer won't be thrilled to see you. You should wait here with Page and Everest. Stacy walked slowly toward the family of deer, keeping her head down and walking a bit sideways so she didn't look like a predator. Perhaps this doe had seen Stacy in the forest before. Or maybe animals had a way of communicating with each other that Stacy didn't know about and she somehow knew Stacy wasn't a threat. Either way, the doe allowed Stacy to approach. Stacy gingerly set the fawn down, bowed to the doe, and walked back to the edge of the clearing where Everest, Basil, and Page were hiding.

Stacy turned around and breathed a huge sigh of relief when she saw the mama deer cleaning the fawn with her tongue. As Stacy and her pack crept away, she snuck one last peek through the trees and saw that the fawn was beginning to nurse.

"Let's go make sure Tucker is safe," Stacy said, eyeing

Page curiously. "Unless you somehow know the location of another animal that needs rescuing?"

Page, obviously oblivious to sarcasm, took the lead, letting them follow her jaunty red tail.

How did you know about the deer and her fawn? There's something strange going on here, and I'm going to figure it out.

ELEVEN

THAT NIGHT, AFTER all the wolves were safe and accounted for back at the cave, Stacy fixed supper, cracking a few of Fluff's freshly laid eggs over the wolves' stew for a change. Without a rooster, Stacy didn't need to candle each egg to see if there was life inside. She would need a rooster eventually, but that was a problem for another day.

After everyone had eaten, Stacy sat down to write her journal entry for the day. She added a quick sketch of Page standing next to the fawn with bats flying around them. Even with today's success, she was worried about what would happen next.

Had the hunters who killed the doe been out here look-ing for wolves? Or had the Village Council voted down the wolf bounty? We can't relax until we know for sure.

She wondered, not for the first time, how she could be one of them—humans. The animals in the forest lived and worked together in a beautiful ecosystem. And yes, death was part of that. Stacy knew nature could be cruel. She knew some animals killed others for food. And she also knew that some humans killed animals for food because she was one of those humans. She fished for salmon in the rivers and slaughtered the chickens from her farm. But Stacy always followed the laws of the taiga. She never took more than she needed and the nourishment she gained from the kills fueled her on her rescue missions. She was part of the forest ecosystem. But the villagers that visited the taiga were not. No matter how hard she tried, Stacy couldn't make sense of some of their actions. They had leveled a great swath of the forest for the electrical sub-station, and then shot at the wild creatures for trespassing on "their" land. They camped out and left piles of gar-bage with no regard for the animals and the trees and the plants. And the worst part was they acted entitled—like the forest belonged to them more than it did to the wolves and the deer and the rabbits and even the bats.

The forest belongs to the wild animals who live here, not

to the humans who show up to take what they want from it and leave.

Page's behavior was getting to be almost as big a mystery to Stacy as the humans were. She was still trying to puzzle out how the sweet, little dog had known about the doe and her fawn. She knew from some of her nature books that dogs have a powerful sense of smell, but it wasn't more powerful than that of her wolves.

So how did Page lead us directly to the doe and then to her fawn?

She finished her journal entry with questions still swirling in her mind. She walked toward the front of the cave to let Wink know it was his turn to patrol the ridge that night.

The moon was just coming up over the treetops when two bats whizzed past Stacy's head from the back of the cave and flew out into the night. Instinctively, Stacy brought both her arms up above her, spun around, and ducked.

WHY ARE THERE SO MANY DANG BATS HERE? Stacy thought as she nonchalantly brought her arms from her face to her hair and pretended like she had just been adjusting her ponytail. Everest wasn't buying it. Amused, he looked at her from his spot in front of the fire.

"Hang on," Stacy said, following the bats outside and into the small clearing in front of the cave's entrance. "The bats showed up when Page did, didn't they? Page, where are you?" Page was standing in the middle of the clearing with a small colony of bats zipping around her. As far as Stacy could tell, the same few bats were swooping around Page, and the dog's ears twitched back and forth, like radio antennae, constantly repositioning themselves to get a better signal. She was listening!

"Page, can you communicate with the bats?" Stacy asked. "Did they tell you about the doe and the fawn?"

Page gave her a little yip, which could have been a yes or a no, and then went back to listening to the bats.

"Addi!" Stacy called. "Bring me the book with the information about bats!"

Addison raced to the back of the cave with Stacy on her heels to search for the right book. At last they found it, tucked in the back of the crammed bookshelf where Fluff was roosting, and Stacy turned to the appropriate page.

"'Bats locate prey through echolocation,'" she read out loud. "'They emit sound waves and listen for an echo to bounce off insects and other objects. Echolocation enables bats to "see" even on the darkest nights. In fact, many species of bats have very poorly developed eyes. They see with their ears instead.'"

The other wolves had gathered around Stacy and Addison to listen.

"There's something going on," Stacy told them. "Something to do with Page and how she knew about the fawn. I think the bats might have told her."

Stacy flipped the pages until she found the section on bat communication.

"'Bats don't just use echolocation to navigate and to catch prey,'" Stacy read. "'They rely on echolocation for communication as well. The noises they make are at such a high frequency that humans can't hear them, but bats are constantly using echolocation to communicate within their own colonies and with other bat colonies.

"'Animals, like dolphins, whales, and some birds, also use echolocation to navigate, hunt, and communicate,'" Stacy continued.

She put down the book and looked around her at the wolves. "I think Page is one of those other animals," she said. "It's not a skill most dogs have, but Page is special in other ways. She understands me—"

Wink interrupted her with a quiet *yip*.

Stacy smiled and scratched Wink behind the ears. "Yes, I know you can understand me, too. You're the most special wolves in the whole world."

Wink gave her a satisfied smirk and Stacy headed toward the front of the cave again. She stood in the shadows watching Page and the bats. They were communicating—of that Stacy was sure.

"Page can talk to the bats," Stacy said to the others. Stacy's mind was racing. *They must have told Page about the doe and her fawn. They could tell Page about animals all over the forest that need our help. We could rescue so many more animals! And not just in our forest. Bats can fly long distances AND they can talk with other colonies in the surrounding biomes, meaning . . .* "Our rescue radius just got much, much bigger!"

The next few days were quiet while Stacy continued to observe Page and the bats. With nightly information from the bat colonies, the possibilities for helping animals in need suddenly seemed boundless.

"We've always been limited to the rescues we stumbled upon," Stacy said to Everest one night when they were working on the farm. "Now the bats can tell us where we're really needed."

The other wolves were up to the task, but it was Addison who reminded Stacy of the practicalities. One night, as Stacy was excitedly talking about all the good they could do, not just in their own forest but beyond, Addison grabbed a book in her teeth and dropped it at Stacy's feet.

"*Overnight Backpacking for Beginners,*" Stacy read. "You're right as always, Addison. If we're going to travel longer distances, we'll have to be ready. I'll pack a rescue bag with everything we need. We could get called away on missions that last a couple of days—or even longer."

Over the next week, Stacy gathered all the emergency essentials. With Wink's help, she laid everything out on the floor of the cave, ready to fill a couple of wolf packs. There was dried fruit and jerky, various containers filled with water, a makeshift first aid kit filled with items they'd compiled from campsites, some extra clothes for Stacy, two torches that were ready to light, waterproof matches, and two of their strong, handmade ropes. Lastly, she added a tarp some hunters had left behind. They could use it as shelter in rain or snow. Stacy stood up and proudly surveyed the assortment of supplies.

"We're ready," she announced to Page and the wolves. "Bring on the rescues!"

TWELVE

SPRING WAS BEGINNING to edge into summer. Stacy had just assumed they'd wait for the bats to let Page know whenever an animal was in trouble. Then a small complication occurred to her.

"Page, how are we going to know if a rescue will take a day, a weekend, or a whole week?" Stacy asked the dog. "You can't tell us where we're going."

Addison was listening and had an idea. She dashed over to a world atlas on Stacy's bookshelf.

Stacy loved looking at maps of different countries around the world. She especially loved the terrain maps that showed forest and desert and mountain regions. But she didn't see how the old atlas could be useful to their rescue plans. "There isn't a map of our forest in that book," she said. "Or if it is there, it's too small to help us."

Addison sat and looked up at her.

"What?" Stacy asked.

The wolf rolled a piece of chalk in Stacy's direction.

"Oh, I get it!" Stacy said. "We'll make our own map and Page can point to where we need to go."

Addison jumped and twisted in the air and let out a woof of delight. Page copied her.

Stacy cracked up at the look of pride on both their faces.

"Okay," she said, gathering a few pieces of different color chalk. "Paints would be better, but chalk will have to do for now." She stopped Addison as she was about to run out of the cave. "No stealing paint from the village, Addi," she said in a stern voice. "The last thing we need is another wolf sighting there."

Sheepishly, Addison tiptoed back into the cave.

Stacy had studied the area around them from the top of the ridge often enough to draw a map from memory. She drew the cave and their small clearing in the center. All around it was the taiga and their ridge with the birch forest, the horrible power substation, the swamp, the ravine, the oak forest, and the rest in the distance.

Everest and Noah trotted in and sat on either side of Stacy, admiring her work.

"It's good, isn't it?" Stacy said. "That's our world."

Addison added a few landmarks that Stacy had missed—details like the waterfall, the wild wolves' den, and the clearing near the river that campers liked to frequent.

Stacy covered that area with an X. *Stay Away,* she wrote. *Humans.*

Addison, likewise, drew a similar X over an area of the

dense forest on the tall mountains north of the swamp, the Forest of Perpetual Darkness.

Everest, who had been watching casually, stiffened and sat up. Noah eyed him uneasily.

"What's the deal with that place, Addi?" Stacy asked. "We never go there, but I'm pretty sure it's too rugged for most humans. We should explore it sometime, don't you think?"

Of course, Stacy understood why they hadn't been before. The mountains were steep and cold, and the trees grew so dense that they swallowed up the daylight. At midday, with the sun at its highest, the forest still felt like it was night. There was something else, too—the memory of a burning smell whenever she thought about it. But, again, when she reached for it, it was just a wisp.

Stacy shook her head, convinced she was confusing two memories. She was sure the wolves hadn't taken her there in the past because she was little and it was the sort of forest that might frighten her. But she was older now and up for the adventure. Stacy reckoned it would be one of their most thrilling expeditions yet. Walking through it, she'd barely be able to see her hand in front of her. And she'd need to sharpen her axe so she could cut through the vines. The wolves with their keen eyesight and thick coats wouldn't have the same issues.

She waited for Addison to scratch something into the dirt of the cave floor—something to make Stacy understand their reservations about the area. The wolf only eyed her with an innocent expression.

"It's a creepy place, isn't it?" Stacy relented, reaching out to scratch behind Addison's ears. "Okay, we'll stay away."

Everyone seemed to relax after that and Stacy went back to adding details to the map. There was plenty of room to expand it as they explored farther afield with the help of Page and the bats.

The next morning, the bat colony that had taken up residence in the cave swooped around Page just like they had on the morning of the fawn rescue. Bats flying during the day was highly unusual. They must have something important to communicate.

Stacy grabbed her satchel while Basil and Everest ran over to the emergency packs. Stacy helped the wolves put them on and waited for Page to use the map to show where they needed to go.

As soon as the bats settled down, Page pointed to a spot on the map not far away, but dangerously close to the campers' clearing by the river.

"No doubt a problem caused by campers," Stacy muttered to herself. She was a little disappointed that this rescue wouldn't take them into new territory, but she never turned down an opportunity to help an animal in need.

If nothing else, Noah would be able to catch some trout for dinner since they would be close to the river.

They raced through the taiga and into the birch forest, slowing as they heard the sound of the river in front of them. And not only the sound of the river, but the sound of human voices. Just as Stacy had suspected. . . .

"Everest and Basil, you need to hang back," Stacy whispered. "We can't have any humans see you, especially since you're wearing packs. That'll raise all kinds of questions."

She scaled a sturdy tree to try to get a better look at what was happening and that was when she saw them: two humans, a man and a woman. The woman had long black hair and brown skin and was about a foot taller than Stacy. She wore a maroon tank top and khaki shorts with hiking boots. The man was even taller and had light brown wavy hair; his skin looked slightly sunburned. He was wearing a plaid shirt and jeans. He must have just bathed in the river—his hair was damp, he had shaving cream on his face, and wasn't wearing any shoes. They were chasing a skunk around their campsite.

Stacy shook her head in disgust. *Serves you right if you get sprayed.* Then she saw *why* they were chasing the frightened creature—its head was stuck in some kind of plastic container. It would starve if someone didn't free it.

Then she saw a group of about six skunk kittens in a burrow just to the north of the clearing. "A surfeit of skunks," she whispered to herself, remembering the term from one of her animal books. They were too young to survive on their own. The skunk and her babies could die, all because a couple of humans were careless with their garbage.

What's the collective noun for people? She hoped it was something awful. *A murder of humans, perhaps, like a murder of crows? Or maybe an unkindness? Like an unkindness of ravens. That would certainly be fitting.*

She slid down the tree trunk and crouched in the middle of the wolf pack. "There's a skunk in trouble," she whispered, "but there are two humans in the way. We'll have to lie low and hope it can get away from them. Let's wait—"

The word wait wasn't even all the way out of Stacy's

mouth before Page took off, running straight for the campsite.

The next thing Stacy heard was the woman's voice. "Hey, little one! Where'd you come from? Are you lost?"

Oh no, Stacy thought, *those humans have Page!*

THIRTEEN

STACY COULDN'T BELIEVE it. Why had Page run to those humans? The last thing Stacy needed was humans messing everything up. They had already done enough damage to the skunk. What if they captured Page?

"Hide," Stacy whispered urgently to Everest and the others. "They can't see you."

The wolves quietly backed away, slinking under vegetation and behind trees. Their fur, in various shades of white and gray, blended into the trunks of the birch trees. Even Stacy had trouble seeing them despite knowing they were there. Everest stayed the closest, ever ready to protect Stacy if she needed him, while the others remained within whistle distance.

Stacy shinnied back up the tree as quietly as she could to find out what was happening with Page. *Did Page run to those humans because she wanted them to take her home? Does she have a human family that she misses? Or has she forgotten her humans the way I've forgotten mine?*

Stacy peeked between the leaves to see Page running around the skunk, forcing it to move closer and closer to the humans. Stacy's horror gave way to a tiny smile when both the woman and Page were forced to jump back to avoid getting sprayed. But the skunk, blinded by the plastic container stuck on its snout, missed them.

The man used the distraction to approach the skunk from the front. He squatted in front of it and grabbed the fur on the mama's back with one hand.

Stacy wanted to scream, *Don't hurt it! It's only protecting itself and its babies! It's* your *human garbage that's the problem.*

But she bit her lip, watching and waiting. She didn't know what she expected—for the man to hit the skunk? For him to throw her into the river or against the trees? Humans were erratic. That much she did know. But this human surprised her. He held the squirming skunk with one hand, reaching for the plastic container with the other, and then he yanked until the plastic cup came off with a popping sound.

The man fell back onto his heels and then onto his butt. The skunk was stunned for a minute. Even from her distance Stacy could see that she was taking fast, shallow breaths while trying to get her bearings. Stacy held her own breath while the woman slowly backed away with Page at her side.

The man didn't or couldn't move. After a few very long, slow seconds the frightened skunk turned and ran, but not before she lifted her tail and sprayed him right in the face. If Stacy wasn't so worried about Page, she might have burst out laughing.

Which is exactly what the female camper did. She started to laugh and was soon laughing so hard that she fell to her knees. The man grabbed a water bottle and poured its contents over his face. Then he took his shirt off and ran to the river and jumped in.

"It's going to take a lot more than water to get that smell off!" the woman shouted, throwing him what appeared to be a bar of soap. "You're going to have to burn those clothes, too."

The man dove underwater and then popped up again, spraying a steady stream of water through his teeth. "Ugh, I can even taste it," he said. He stood and started to splash her.

The woman jumped out of the way with a scream, then sat a few feet away from the splash zone.

"At least you got the plastic off her," the woman said. "Otherwise she would've starved to death, poor thing."

The man shook his head. "If careless people wouldn't leave their garbage behind, that never would have happened."

Wait, it wasn't you? Stacy thought. She had been sure these people were responsible. It surprised her to hear that they were just as disapproving of other humans and their garbage as she was.

Maybe there are some decent humans. I still don't want them coming into my part of the forest, and I certainly don't want them keeping my dog.

It was as if the woman heard her thoughts.

"Now, what are we going to do about this little guy?" she asked, putting an arm around Page. She rubbed Page's belly with the other hand. "Um, I mean girl."

She has a family! Stacy answered silently. *Just let her go.*

That's what she would expect most humans to do, whether the dog was tame or wild. But these humans were different. They appeared to genuinely care.

"We can bring her to the village," the man said. He was still in the river soaping himself and his clothes.

(Stacy knew from experience that soap would barely take the edge off the scent. It would stick to him for a few days at least. The clothes would take longer, but if they were washed, rolled in pine needles, and then washed again and left in the sunshine they might eventually lose their sharp scent.) "Maybe someone there knows where it belongs," he added.

"Maybe she belongs with us," the woman said, now scratching Page's ears affectionately. "She's a smart dog, and I can tell she likes me."

"You can't save every stray you come across," the man said, chuckling.

"Said by the man who got sprayed saving a skunk," the woman shot back.

The man tried to splash her again, but the woman was too far away.

Stacy watched as Page started to trot to the edge of the clearing. She must have realized her work was done: the skunk was saved, the man was climbing out of the river, and the woman had finished giving her a rub.

Stacy slid down the tree as noiselessly as she could. Motioning to Everest to stay put, she knelt at the edge of the clearing and waited for Page. *We'll slip off before the woman sees me.*

"Here, girl! Here, girl!" the woman called after Page.

She ran over to her camping gear and grabbed a granola bar. "Food! Want a treat?"

Stacy saw Page lick her lips in anticipation. The dog turned and ran back to the woman.

No, Page! Stacy shook her head. She knew Page wouldn't be able to resist the sugary snack after weeks of subsisting on only pumpkin and fish.

While Page was gobbling up pieces of granola bar, Stacy noticed the woman was fashioning a leash from her rope belt. *Where are the bats when I need them? They could warn Page about the leash.*

In a moment of inspiration, Stacy let out a whistle, hoping Page would hear it and run to her. Page's ears twitched, but it was too late. The woman had slipped the lead over Page's head. Page strained against the leash, but the woman wouldn't let go. Page was trapped.

Stacy felt waves of panic start to wash over her body. She didn't know what to do, but she did know she couldn't lose Page—she was Stacy's dog now, had taken up a place in her pack and her heart.

Stacy took a deep breath and stepped into the clearing. She didn't remember ever talking to another human before, but she no longer had a choice.

"Hey," she said, her voice trembling. "That's my dog."

FOURTEEN

THE WOMAN GREETED Stacy with a big smile. "Aw, she's a great dog! What's her name?"

"Page," Stacy answered. "Like pages in a book." Her own voice sounded strange, scratchy and hollow. She talked to the wolves all the time, but never to humans. She was suddenly self-conscious about the way she sounded.

"Does she like to read?" the man asked with a laugh. He had finally finished rinsing off and was climbing back up the riverbank, wearing now wet jeans and flip-flops. His dripping hair was sticking up in spikes all over his head.

The woman laughed, too. "Don't mind him; he likes to tease. And I recommend you stay upwind. He just got sprayed by a skunk."

Stacy tried to smile, but judging by the woman's reaction it wasn't a natural smile. *I probably look like a frightened deer. If only I could run away like one.*

Out of the corner of her eye she saw Everest moving closer to the edge of the clearing. She held up her hand to let him know everything was okay.

"I'm guessing you're the one who likes to read?" the woman said.

Stacy nodded.

"Do you have any favorites?"

Stacy just wanted to get Page and leave, but the woman still had a hold of her makeshift leash.

"Favorite books?" Stacy asked.

"Yeah, what do you like to read?"

The name of every book she had ever read flew out of Stacy's head. "*Island of the Blue Dolphins*," she answered finally. She walked closer to the woman, reaching out for Page.

"Oh, I loved that one when I was your age," the woman said. "What grade are you in?"

"Grade?"

"In school."

Stacy's mind raced. She had no idea what grade most twelve-year-olds were in. She knew they moved up year after year. She couldn't remember if the numbers went up or down for that. Then a phrase from a newspaper article popped into her mind. "I'm homeschooled," she said.

The man came toward them, still smelling like skunk stink.

"Ugh." The woman waved her hand under her nose. "Change those clothes at once."

The man saluted her and stepped into their tent.

Stacy reached for Page again. Page yipped and wagged her tail.

"Well, I should—"

But the woman had more questions. "Are you from the village? Or are you camping nearby?"

Stacy gave a vague wave past the clearing. "Over there," she said.

"Funny," the woman said. "Yesterday we walked a lot in that area collecting garbage and didn't see any other campers."

Stacy could feel her face heating up. She had read about blushes in books. Was that what she was doing? Would the woman know she was lying?

"Umm, we just got here," Stacy said. "And Page ran

off first thing. But, wait, you were collecting garbage?"

The woman shrugged. The man came out of the tent, wearing clean clothes and holding his others at arm's length. Stacy eyed them. The pants would be way too big on her but she could cut them down into shorts and weave a vine thorough the belt loops to hold them up. The shirt would come in handy, too. But he dropped both into a fire pit. There was no flame now, but it was all set up for a nice blaze.

He'll probably burn them before one of the wolves can come back for them. Too bad.

"We come a couple of times a year. It's our own personal cleanup effort," the man said. "Although now with this wolf bounty—"

Stacy's heart sank. "Wait, they passed that?" she asked. Stacy tried to keep the panic out of her voice, but her heart, which was already beating fast, sped up even more.

"They did and it's terrible," the man said. "The wolves are only doing what they need to do to survive."

"So the bounty, it's already happening?" Stacy gulped.

"It takes effect in a few days," the woman said. "You won't have to worry about them during your trip. But if you're going to be in the forest later this year you'll need to be careful—wear bright colors, watch out for hunters."

"I will," Stacy said, her mind already racing. *I can keep myself safe, but what about my wolves? We have to go into hiding right NOW.*

"The council said they were going to set aside protected areas for campers, but that's hard to enforce. Local farmers are determined to kill as many wolves as possible," the man added. "We've been camping here for years and never had a wolf encounter. They're usually frightened by humans."

"It's so beautiful out here," the woman continued. "We found this spot when we were staying in town to protest the substation last year. But campers always leave garbage behind. Every time we come we fill up three or four bags of trash and carry them out with us."

All Stacy wanted to do was get Page and run—warn the wolves about what was coming and head underground—but the couple had caught her attention with their talk of garbage cleanup. She figured she could spare a few more minutes to talk with them. "Wow," Stacy said. "I didn't know humans did that."

The man cocked his head and gave her a sly grin. "Humans? Are you one of us or are you another species altogether?"

Oh, jeez, I guess humans don't refer to each other as

humans. To cover her mistake, she blurted out, "You protested the substation?"

"We were in the village every weekend for about six months. We had a lot of people on our side, but in the end the energy companies won and the forest lost."

Stacy nodded. "It's really ugly. And lots of animals lost their homes."

"It'll be even uglier if these developers get their way," he said.

"Wait, what?" Stacy asked. "Developers?"

"A big development firm wants to build a luxury resort—golf course, swimming pools and spas, hunting and fishing lodges. You name it, they want it," he said.

"But what about the forest?" Stacy asked weakly.

"They're asking for rights to the whole area—the taiga, the birch forest, the river, even the hills will become ski slopes," the woman said.

"They can't!" Stacy said. She wanted to scream: *This is my home. This is my wolves' home.* But of course she couldn't. All of a sudden Stacy felt as if all the blood in her body had rushed to her head. Her ears started ringing. It was so loud she wondered if the humans could hear it, and then she suddenly got dizzy.

She fell to her knees. *I'm going to lose my home.*

FIFTEEN

"ARE YOU ALL right?" The woman was leading Stacy to a camp chair. "You looked like you blacked out for a second there."

Stacy took some deep breaths. *In and out,* she reminded herself. *In and out.* "I'm fine," she said. "I didn't know about—"

"Aw, you must really love it here," the woman said. "You've probably been coming here since you were little, yeah?"

"It might not even happen," the man assured her. "We're going to fight it, and a lot of people will join us.

We can't let greedy businesses destroy the whole planet."

"You'll join us, right?" the woman said to Stacy with a smile. "You're going to leave your campsite as pristine as it was when you found it, yes? Take all your garbage out with you?"

Stacy would have laughed at the idea of her and the wolves messing up the forest if she wasn't suddenly so worried about the wolf bounty and now this plan to steal the land. "Definitely," she said. "Now I'd better get Page—"

"She really should have a collar," the woman said. "With your contact info, in case she runs off again."

"I . . . we . . . have one, but it's at home," Stacy said, lying again.

The woman took her belt from around Page's neck and the dog danced over to Stacy wagging her tail.

"Feel free to come over here with your parents tonight," the man said. "We're going to make s'mores. We've got more than enough."

"S'mores?"

"Oh my gosh, how have you never had s'mores?" the woman asked.

Stacy eyed her, confused.

"Graham crackers and chocolate bars and roasted

marshmallows—put together like a sandwich," the woman said. "They're so good you want some more—s'mores! You have to come back with your parents tonight and try one."

Stacy hesitated. How could she say yes and then show up without her imaginary parents?

The woman mistook Stacy's hesitation for something else. "I'm Miriam, by the way," she said, reaching her hand toward Stacy.

Stacy didn't know what she was supposed to do at first. She nearly backed up. Then she remembered pictures in the newspaper of politicians shaking people's hands. She wiped her hand on her jeans and reached out to shake.

"And that's Jack," the woman said, pointing to the guy who was likely her boyfriend or husband.

He came closer, ready to shake, too, but Miriam waved him back. "Stay out of smelling distance until you've had at least one more bath. Maybe two."

He cupped his hands around his mouth like he was shouting from a great distance. "We'd love to have you and your family for s'mores," he yelled.

Stacy smiled. *These humans—no,* people *is the word I should use—are way different than I expected. They're nice. And they fight for the forest.*

Suddenly, more than anything, Stacy wanted to sit around a fire with them and talk about how to fight against wolf bounties and substations and plans to turn the forest into a playground while they ate these exotic-sounding graham cracker sandwiches with—*what was in them again?*—chocolate toastmallows. But there would be too many awkward questions about parents and campsites and what a young girl like her was doing out alone in the forest.

"I would," Stacy said, her voice cracking, "but we're leaving as soon as I get back with Page."

"But I thought you just got here," Jack said, his forehead wrinkled in confusion. "Didn't you say that?"

Did she? Stacy felt her face getting hot again. She'd forgotten that she told them she had just arrived. "I . . . uh . . . we . . . just came for an afternoon hike," Stacy stammered. "We have to be home tonight."

The woman seemed to be studying her carefully and Stacy started to panic.

"I'd better get back. They'll be worried," she said, edging away.

"Okay, nice meeting you," Miriam said.

"Bye," Stacy answered. "C'mon, Page." She turned and forced herself to move at a normal pace. There was something about the way Miriam was looking at her that made Stacy uneasy. It was like she knew there wasn't a human family waiting for her. It was all Stacy could do not to run, but she was afraid that would make the woman even more suspicious.

"Hey, wait!" Jack yelled.

Stacy started to run.

"You didn't tell us your name."

"It's Stacy!" she said over her shoulder.

"Bye, Stacy!"

Stacy had reached the edge of the clearing, Page scampering behind her. She stepped from the bright sunlight into the shade of the trees, blinking. Everest was nearby, ready to do whatever she needed. Stacy made sure Jack and Miriam couldn't see her and then crouched for a moment, petting him and the other wolves while her pounding heart settled back to a normal rhythm.

She wasn't sure why, but she found herself needing to know what Miriam and Jack were saying about her. She crept around the edge of the clearing, making sure she was hidden by the trees and the undergrowth, and found a spot within earshot of the couple.

The two humans were still in the middle of the clearing near their fire pit.

"Something's off," Miriam was saying. "Something is wrong and she didn't want to tell us. Why is she wandering around in the woods alone? She looked like she hadn't had a bath in a while, either."

"She wasn't alone. She was with her dog. I'm sure her parents were nearby."

"Not so nearby that they could hear us talking," Miriam said. "We could have been kidnappers. She was so awkward, though. And did you see the way she got scared when you talked about the developer?"

Jack shook his head. "She loves the forest like we do, and she's a kid who was confronted by two strangers in the woods who had her dog. You'd be a little awkward, too, if that happened to you. Plus, she said she was home-schooled. Maybe she doesn't spend a lot of time talking to adults beside her parents."

"I don't know . . ." Miriam said. "I have a weird feeling about the whole thing. Maybe we should look for her. Make sure there are parents. I want to be sure she's taken care of."

Stacy's heart started hammering again. *The first thing humans will do if they find out about me is make me leave my wolf family in the forest. If there's still a forest to leave, anyway.*

Jack shook his head. "Of course she has parents, Miriam, what are you talking about? And she looked perfectly clean to me. She was polite. She likes reading. She's just a normal kid who's a bit wary of strangers, that's all. The only thing that was genuinely weird about her is that she'd never heard of s'mores. That's just wrong."

Miriam bit her lip and went back to starting their fire, seeming to accept Jack's explanation for Stacy's behavior.

Stacy crawled backward away from the clearing, confused and filled with conflicting feelings. She was relieved they hadn't decided to come looking for her fake parents. She was also a little embarrassed that Miriam had thought her odd, but proud at the same time because even though she had been really uncomfortable, and a bit awkward, Stacy had survived her first human interaction (first in a long time, at least) and successfully retrieved Page. The feeling that confused her the most was that there was just a hint of a longing to spend more time with the couple. And it wasn't only because she wanted to taste s'mores and find out more about the proposed development; she liked hearing the two of them talk. She liked the fact that they fought against the substation and had warned her about the bounty, and she liked that they loved animals, even skunks. And Stacy liked that they cleaned up the garbage other humans left behind. She liked *them*. And that was confusing because, up until this point, Stacy had been so sure that she didn't like any of her own kind.

But the feeling Stacy felt that overtook all the others—bigger than the relief of getting Page back or the confusion over enjoying her interaction with the humans—was fear. Pure fear. The village vote to reinstate a wolf bounty had passed and that meant that in a few days' time, hunters would be coming into the forest with the express purpose of killing wolves. And not just the wild wolves that were killing the farmer's sheep . . . *her* wolves. At any moment, a hunter could shoot one of her wolves.

SIXTEEN

"WE'RE GOING INTO hiding until this blows over."

Stacy was back in the cave with Page and the pack explaining the wolf bounty.

"I mean, I guess we've always been in hiding," she continued. "But this time it's serious. Everything to the west of our cave is off-limits, okay? It's too close to the village. Supposedly there will be protected areas for campers, which hunters have to avoid. But the rest of the forest is open ground for them and what they want is to find wolves."

Stacy stood in front of the cave entrance with Everest and Basil looking down at a very glum Wink, Addison,

Tucker, and Noah. Page was napping near the back of the cave.

"They want to *kill* you," Stacy said in a forceful tone. She hated speaking so harshly to the wolves, but the stakes were too high now. "No one is to leave the cave during the day, do you understand me?"

Stacy's wolves were crepuscular, just like normal wolves in the wild, meaning they were most active at dawn and dusk. Stacy's pack had retrained their body clocks to accommodate her sleep schedule, but now that the bounty was in full force, they'd need to change their behavior again.

"We'll gather food at night, using the buddy system," Stacy continued. "Everest, your buddy is Tucker. Basil, you're with Addison. Wink and Noah, that means you guys are buddies. And Page, you can be with me."

The wolves stood up and got into their pairings. Stacy could tell they were disappointed. This time of year in the taiga usually meant long hikes to pick blackberries, endless games of tag at twilight, and water fights in the river. None of that was going to happen.

"It's going to be a rough summer," Stacy warned them. "And one more thing," she added looking in Page's direction, "all rescue missions are suspended until further notice."

Over the next two weeks, Stacy and the pack stuck to Stacy's plan of staying in the cave during the day and foraging for food at night. It was strange for Stacy to sleep snuggled with all six of the wolves, but she enjoyed not having to worry about one of them patrolling the ridge alone every night.

The long days spent inside the cave were punctuated by gunshots. Stacy flinched every time she heard one and noted it in her daily diary entry. She'd been spending all her free time (and she had lots of it now) on a new wood-crafting project: a beautiful wooden chest. She was sanding down some of the planks for the top of the chest when another gunshot rang out in the forest.

"That's seven," she said solemnly, standing up to walk over to her desk.

Stacy wondered how many of those bullets had hit their intended targets. As much as she hoped all of them had missed, she knew that wasn't statistically likely. Dusky's pack was being culled and there was nothing Stacy or her wolves could do about it.

"I need some fresh air," Stacy announced to the others. She stood up from her desk and grabbed a book and her satchel and started toward the cave exit. She felt a long cry coming on and didn't want the wolves to see that. But Everest stopped her.

"Don't worry, boy," Stacy said, stopping to give him a hug. She showed him the book in her hand. "I'm only going a little way out to forage for mushrooms. According to our cookbook, they are great in an omelet."

Everest shook his head.

"No one's going to shoot me," Stacy said reassuringly. "It's you they're looking for. Besides, I think I can talk my way out of any chance encounter with humans now that I practiced with Jack and Miriam."

Before Everest could stop her again, Stacy pulled back the branch trapdoor they'd moved from the farm to the cave when they first went into hiding. Stacy was much more concerned with hunters finding them than finding her pumpkin patch, so she'd thought it best to have the strongest members of the pack, Everest and Noah, help her carry it from her farm to the cave and lean it upright against the cave opening.

Once out, she shimmied past the basketball-size boulders they'd rolled up all around the cave's entry.

"I'll be gone an hour at most," she whispered back into the cave. It wasn't directed at any wolf in particular, but Stacy knew their hearing was good enough that all of them would hear her. "If I'm gone longer, DO NOT come looking for me. I'll be fine."

Stacy walked south for a little while in the hot summer sun, occasionally glancing behind her to make sure none of her wolves had been foolish enough to follow her. Then she turned to the right and headed west in the direction of the village. She wasn't entirely sure what she was on the lookout for, but she knew she wanted to see if she could spot any clues as to what had been happening in her beloved taiga while they'd been in hiding. Warm tears started streaming down her cheeks while she walked, as she imagined Dusky's pack being thinned. *No animal deserves to die just because they were acting on their natural instincts. Why do humans think they're more deserving of the forest just because they have guns and can—*

Stacy's thoughts were interrupted by a bright yellow contraption she suddenly found herself face-to-face with. It had three legs and was about as tall as she was and had a type of a telescope mounted on the top of the tripod, but there was no telescope tube. Stacy had no idea what it was used for or who had left it here. She walked up and inspected it.

THEODOLITE 86–100:
PROPERTY OF COUNTY SURVEYOR
DO NOT MOVE

Stacy didn't understand what some of the words meant. And there was nothing else around it that helped her to piece together why this odd piece of equipment had been placed in the taiga.

"Jim, I'm heading back to the east point near the golf pro shop."

Stacy whipped around to see a man in an orange vest

walking in her direction. Luckily his head was turned away from Stacy as he called out to whoever Jim was, which gave her the seconds she needed to dart behind the largest spruce tree she could find.

What golf shop was he talking about? Stacy wondered from behind the tree as the man walked up to the tripod and looked into its telescope. Suddenly she understood. These men were working on the proposed development, sizing up the taiga like it was already theirs. Stacy fought the sudden urge to run out from behind the tree and kick over the theodolite. She still had no idea what a theodolite was, but if it were being used to help plan the development, she'd lose no sleep if it were to accidentally break.

Rather than stick around and get angrier, Stacy turned on her heels and walked quickly back toward the cave. Her trip outside the cave had accomplished the opposite of what it was meant to do. Instead of finding answers and allowing her to clear her mind and come to terms with what was happening to the wild wolves, Stacy's brain was now cluttered with more confusion and hurt than ever. *Even if the wolf bounty ends, now they had this new threat to their home to deal with. What if Miriam and Jack were unsuccessful in their fight against the development? What would happen to Stacy and her wolves when the construction crews came to clear the forest? Would they have to leave the taiga forever? Where would they go?*

Everest was waiting by the door to the cave when Stacy got back. He jumped up, an obvious look of relief flashing across his face.

"Told you I wouldn't be gone long," Stacy said, giving him a pat and setting down her bag. Everest sniffed the bag and then gave her a quizzical look.

"Oh, um," Stacy started. "Yeah, I couldn't find any mushrooms . . . none that I thought were edible, at least. The rabbits must have eaten all the ones around here."

It was the first time Stacy had lied to Everest and she felt horrible about it.

As everyone dug into their evening meal, Stacy looked around the cave and realized the morale of the group was at an all-time low. Everest was worried, probably because he could tell how worried Stacy was, even while she was trying to hide it. Noah was exhausted from having to fish every night to keep the group fed. He kept nodding off into his dinner bowl and then jerking his head up when it dipped too low into his fish stew. Basil was getting stir-crazy, a result of not being able to run free as much as before. Tucker and Addison were heartbroken they couldn't go on rescue missions. Tucker was especially upset over the gunshots they'd been hearing.

He was Stacy's most sensitive wolf, after all, so the idea of any animal being hunted affected him more than the others. And as for Wink, well, he was mostly just bored. To that end, Stacy decided to break out a special book Addison had brought her a few months ago that Stacy had been saving for a stormy, drizzly day when they were trapped inside. There hadn't been any of those recently, though. In fact, it hadn't rained in weeks, which was unusual even in the summer for the taiga. But rain or not, they were definitely stuck inside, so this was as good a time as any for Stacy to start reading it aloud to the pack at night.

The book was about a boy wizard at a magical school and all the wolves really seemed to be enjoying it. Except for Noah, who had fallen into a deep sleep the minute they'd all curled up to read the book.

Stacy had just gotten to an exciting chapter about a troll when she was interrupted by a flurry of bats that flew up from the back of the cave. Stacy tried to ignore them, but they had formed a circle around Page, her ears twitching wildly in an effort to understand their signals. Suddenly Page was jumping at Stacy's feet, tugging her bootlaces toward the cave map.

"I know it's after dark, but we still can't risk going

out, Page," Stacy said. A couple of weeks ago, when one of the seven gunshots had woken them up in the middle of the night, Stacy realized the evenings were not as safe as she'd thought. She had scaled back their nightly excursions to quick trips to and from the river so Noah could fish. Every other night, they went with all the wolves to create a defensive perimeter while Noah fished. But they'd gone last night, so tonight they were meant to stay inside the cave.

Page did not seem to care about these rules, however, and was pulling on Stacy even more frantically. Humoring the little dog, Stacy made her way over to look at the map. She had no intention of taking the wolves out of the cave on a rescue mission. For all she knew, the bats were telling Page about a hunter closing in on one of the wild wolves. Page could be unknowingly leading them directly into harm's way and that was a risk Stacy was unwilling to take. Her eyebrows raised, however, when she saw where Page was pointing to on the map.

"The Forest of Perpetual Darkness?" Stacy asked, looking down at Page, whose tail was wagging wildly back and forth. *The terrain is so wild there. It's not like the taiga: it's almost impossible to take two steps without having to climb or cut your way through vines. Hunters never enter.* "There's an animal that needs saving there?"

Page nodded vigorously.

Stacy contemplated her options. An animal needed their help in a part of the forest that she knew hunters would not be in. A part of the forest that she herself had not explored much and that would give her restless wolves a chance to stretch their legs.

"Everyone grab your packs," Stacy said loudly. "We're going on a rescue."

SEVENTEEN

STACY, EVEREST, BASIL, Addison, and Tucker raced through the forest after Page and the bats. With no moon out that night, it was completely dark. Stacy rode Basil, who had no trouble navigating through the pitch-black forest with the other wolves. Wink was not pleased when Stacy told him he had to stay at the cave with his buddy Noah, who had still been snoring loudly when the others set off. Rules were rules, though, and Stacy was happy Noah was getting the rest he needed.

They were following the river north toward the falls, when Page and the bats suddenly stopped. Four bats frantically flew in front of each of the wolves' faces, halting them in their tracks. A fifth bat flew up to Stacy and nudged her forward.

"I think this bat wants to show me something up ahead," Stacy said, skeptical. "Wait here, guys, I'm not going to go far."

Stacy hopped off Basil and had only walked about ten feet from the group when she saw it: a steel trap on the forest floor with a few pine branches on either side of it for camouflage. *The villagers really need the bounty that badly?* Rage bubbled up inside her. Setting a trap was crueler than hunting them with guns, which was awful but at least quick. This way, the injured wolf would meet a much more painful end. It would either bleed to death from its injuries, die from dehydration without water, or its wound would get infected and sickness would ravage the wolf's body over the course of several agonizing days. *The wolf would suffer.* That is, if it was even a wolf that set off the trap. Any helpless animal in the taiga could have set off this trap.

Stacy reached into her satchel and pulled out an apple.

"Stand back," she said to the bat. "Or . . . uh, fly back."

The bat flew back a couple feet. Stacy looked around

to make sure her wolves and Page were still a safe distance away and then gently lobbed the apple into the center of the trap. *CRACK*. The trap snapped shut and Stacy shuddered, imagining what would have happened if it had been an animal instead of an apple.

Stacy climbed back onto Basil's back and everyone set off again. Even though Stacy knew the chances of a hunter being in the forest in the middle of the night were slim, she was eager to reach the safe cover of the Forest of Perpetual Darkness. The pack raced through the northernmost tip of the taiga toward the swamplands. Not counting a few water breaks, Stacy estimated about three hours had passed. She realized they had entered the swampland, but it didn't have its usual rotten egg smell. Even though that smell was gross, it did signal that the land was fertile and growing. Its absence was not a good sign. She strained her eyes to see the ground as it passed by quickly beneath Basil's powerful paws. It was dry and devoid of the slimy puddles that were usually everywhere.

I hope we get a good rainstorm soon, Stacy thought. *The forest needs it.*

Page and the bats veered to the left, where the swampland gave way to the tree-covered foothills that made up the base of the steep snowcapped mountain range. Behind them, the sun was rising over the swamp from the east. In front of them, dense trees swallowed every bit of light: the Forest of Perpetual Darkness. Suddenly, Stacy saw a shadow on her left side. It was Everest with a burst of energy, speeding up to overtake Basil and Page. Basil, Addison, and Tucker began to slow down, as if they'd been signaled to do so. Stacy watched as Everest passed Page and then quickly spun around, blocking the dog's path while nipping at the air, stopping the bats in their place. Page tried to find a way around Everest, but the giant wolf blocked her with ease. Unable to keep going, Page circled back to Stacy and started to whimper.

"Why did we stop?" Stacy asked, jumping off Basil's back.

She had been expecting this: ever since Addison had marked the X on the map over this area of the forest, Stacy had wondered what it was about this particular section of their world that seemed to frighten her wolves.

"Listen," she said. "There's an animal in there that needs our help."

Stacy watched as Basil began to pace anxiously back and forth. Addison's amber eyes were wide and intensely staring at Everest, who was looking at Page as if he was trying to relay a message to the dog without Stacy seeing. Tucker was gently nudging Stacy away from the forest edge.

Is there really some unknown danger here I don't know about? Or are they just uneasy about heading into territory we haven't explored before?

"Look, guys," Stacy started. "I really don't think there's anything in there that we can't handle as a team. We've come so far; we can't give up now. Everest, why don't you lead the way *with* Page and if you sense ANY danger at all—if a flower so much as gives you the creeps—we'll follow your lead and get out of there."

This seemed to satisfy Everest, who nodded to Addison, Basil, and Tucker and then allowed Page to lead the way into the dark forest, staying close on her heels. Stacy shivered at the dark task that lay before them. It had been her idea to come on this rescue, but now that they were here, the forest ahead seemed incredibly daunting. If she didn't know an animal was in serious trouble, she'd turn right around and run in the opposite direction. As if they could read her mind, the five bats that were with them flew off into the dawn. Stacy and her pack were on their own now.

They stepped under the rooflike cover of the trees. All signs of daybreak quickly vanished. It might as well have been midnight for how dark it was now. Stacy lit a torch. Suddenly, a new colony of bats found them, whizzing in circles around Page. *Of course,* Stacy thought. *These must be the bats who sent our bats the signal. Thank goodness they found us. Otherwise we'd just be stumbling around in the dark.*

Page's ears twitched this way and that, gathering information. Basil crouched to let Stacy climb on her back and Addison ran in front of the pack to take the lead. Oddly, Everest fell back and took up a position on Stacy's left side. Tucker walked along next to Everest.

That's strange. Normally they'd stand guard on either side of me.

The wolves exchanged nervous glances.

There it is again, Stacy thought. *That uneasiness. What's going on? Do they sense some danger to the west?*

The air grew cold and Stacy was happy to have Basil's thick, warm fur to hold on to. Just as Stacy suspected, the terrain here was steep and rocky, and it was difficult to navigate through the trees.

The bats led the way with Addison jumping over tree roots and scaling rocks. They climbed up, up, up into the forest. Stacy knew it was morning, but it was as dark as the darkest night with no moon and no stars to guide them. Her torch only illuminated a couple of feet in front of them before its light was swallowed up by the trees and the thick vines that hung from their branches and twisted around their trunks. When it burned out, Stacy didn't bother to light another one. Between the bats' echolocation and the wolves' keen night vision, she didn't need to be able to see where they were going. She trusted her animals.

Everest and Tucker kept the group in check, keeping them east of where Addison's X was on the map. They got tense if they had to take even a short detour to the west to avoid a giant rock or a fallen tree.

After forty minutes, everyone was exhausted. Stacy's face was covered in scratches from tree branches that seemed to poke her out of nowhere. They rested again before the final push. Tucker made the rounds tending to Stacy's scratches and making sure no one had been seriously hurt. All too soon, the bats hurried them onward.

The climb was steady, the darkness was unrelenting, and it had been nearly four hours since they left their cozy cave. *How much longer?*

And then she heard it: a weak and eerie grunt.

"We're nearly there!" Stacy said. "I can hear an animal!"

The sound was what they needed for an energy boost. The newly determined pack dove into a thicket of scrub oak with tangled branches and hanging vines. Stacy pulled out her hatchet and started hacking at the vines in front of them. The branches and vines almost seemed like they were alive and trying to get in their way. Stacy could have sworn she saw one move. She blinked her bleary eyes. She *did* see one move. Right in front of her, four brown branches had definitely twitched. Stacy realized what she was looking at. They were legs. Stacy heard a snort above her. She looked up and let out a loud gasp.

There, its antlers caught in a mess of vines and branches, was a moose, staring straight back at her.

EIGHTEEN

STACY LOOKED UP at the frightened moose—his antlers were still covered in velvet and had a couple of points on each side.

"Why, you're just a yearling," Stacy said softly. "It's all right; we won't hurt you. We're here to help."

The moose shifted in place, panic in his eyes. His grunts got louder and more insistent. The wolves lowered themselves to the ground in a gesture that said, *We're not here to attack.*

"They won't hurt you," Stacy said, putting her hand on the moose's side. She could feel his bones. "How long has it been since you've eaten?" she asked.

She poured some water into her hand and held it close to the moose's mouth. His small antlers were so tightly entwined in the vines that the poor thing couldn't even lower his head to drink or eat the vegetation all around him. He lapped up every drop of water and licked all around Stacy's arm, searching for more.

"I don't even want to know what kind of messes I'd get into if I had antlers that started growing out of my head," Stacy said sympathetically to the moose.

That simple act—giving the moose water—was all Stacy needed to earn his trust. The trust extended to the wolves, too. The moose stopped his nervous prancing and stood quietly, as if he knew they were about to rescue him.

Even though he was just a little over a year old, the moose towered over Stacy. She had to stand on Basil's back and hold her torch high to get a good look at the vines. In his attempts to get away, the moose had gotten himself even more tangled. It was going to take a while to cut away the thick vines.

She gently climbed onto the moose's back and reached into her pack for the hunter's knife in its leather pouch. But one look at the tangled vines told her that it would take hours for her to do this job on her own. She needed an extra set of hands, or teeth.

"I'm going to work on the vines closest to the antlers," Stacy told the others. "Addison and Tucker, can you try to chew through the others? Maybe we can untwist some."

She used a loose vine to tie the torch firmly to a branch just over the moose's head and got to work while Addison and Tucker tried to chew through some of the vines.

All of a sudden Stacy heard a crunching noise in the distance. It was growing louder by the second. She looked up from the vines. "Everest, what is th—" Suddenly another moose came into view, crashing through the scrub oak and running directly toward Stacy. It was bigger than the moose Stacy was attempting to rescue. It didn't have antlers, though, so it was able to flatten the forest as it barreled toward Stacy and the pack. *Is it the moose's sibling? Or, worse, its mama?*

"Get back!" Stacy yelled to the wolves and Page. Basil, Addison, Tucker, and Page darted away, but Everest ran toward Stacy, positioning himself directly in front of the charging moose. "Everest, no!"

Stacy braced herself for impact, but the moose pulled up just inches from where Everest was standing. It snorted wildly and then retreated.

"It's going to charge again!" Stacy shouted. "She

doesn't know that we're trying to help. Basil, Everest, you've got to try to distract her. Everyone else . . . START CHEWING!"

Everest and Basil sprung into action, nipping at the moose's legs to confuse her and get her to stop charging. It wasn't the kindest method of subduing the powerful creature, but it worked and gave Stacy and the others the time they needed to free the yearling.

Page was draped over the moose's back, furiously gnawing through the vines at the base of his antlers. Addison was perched on a low branch just at his shoulder, methodically untangling the vines, and Tucker was working on the moose's hooves and also licking the leg wounds the moose had gotten while trying to free himself.

The vines were thick and strong and Stacy's hand began to cramp with the effort. After several minutes, they managed to cut through the thickest vines, and Stacy began to unravel and untwist.

At last he had just one or two small vines wrapped around the base of his left antler. "I'm going to leave those," Stacy told him. "I don't want to cut you and you're going to shed your antlers in the winter anyway. The vines that are left aren't going to hurt you."

The moose cocked its head at her, not understanding.

"You're free now," Stacy told him, rubbing her cramped fingers.

The moose blinked in surprise and shook its head, suddenly understanding it could move. It immediately lowered its head and started to eat the vegetation on the ground. Stacy swung her leg around as she slid down the moose's neck and hopped off. Everest and Basil each took a step back from the moose that had charged Stacy. The two moose walked toward each other and then disappeared together into the dense forest. Exhausted, Stacy leaned against Basil and drew the others around her.

"Thanks, everyone," she said with a yawn. "You've been amazing." She closed her eyes for a second, wondering if she had the energy to begin the long journey home. She was so tired she felt dizzy and was beginning to dream while she was still awake.

"I know this forest is not the nicest place," she said, "but I think we need to rest here for a couple of hours before we start home."

The others were just as tired as she was. Even so, Stacy noticed that Everest and Tucker stayed awake and formed a kind of barrier behind her when she curled up next to Basil. The last thing she remembered before drifting off to sleep was Addison looking west with a fierce expression, as if she expected something to come from that direction.

The forest was so dark that when Stacy woke up she had no idea how long they'd slept and whether it was day or night. She was the last to wake. Everest and Addison were standing over her holding the water canteen and a handful, or rather a pawful, of wild huckleberries. The moose were still nearby, Stacy could hear them munching on some tall grass. Everest nudged Stacy to her feet.

"I guess you're both in a hurry to leave," she said to Everest and Addison, then took a long drink and stuffed all the berries into her mouth. "I agree. Let's get out of here."

The journey down the mountain was easier but felt longer. Even though the forest was dark, Stacy knew it must be morning and she was nervous about returning to their cave in broad daylight. *What if hunters were around looking to cash in on the bounty? Maybe they should wait until nightfall to return.* They were just coming out of the Forest of Perpetual Darkness when a cluster of bats appeared and started whizzing around Page again.

We do NOT have the energy for another rescue right now, Stacy thought.

The bats flew off and Page made some frantic motions to the wolves, who seemed to understand. All at once, everyone starting sprinting toward the taiga. Basil circled back to Stacy and lowered her head, a signal for Stacy to climb on her back.

"What's going on?" Stacy yelled. But then she saw it. *Light up ahead!* By the height of the sun, she guessed it was late morning. "There's daylight!" But her voice caught in her throat when she saw—in the far distance beyond the swamp—their taiga. It was too far away to make out the details of their ridge and the cave below it, but not so far away that Stacy couldn't see the thick smoke that hovered over the treetops.

"FIRE!"

NINETEEN

ANY LINGERING TIREDNESS Stacy, Page, and the wolves felt vanished when they saw their beloved taiga on fire. They raced through the foothills to the swamp. Stacy climbed onto Basil's back while Page rode on Tucker. They were traveling back much faster than their trip out had been, but it still took several agonizing hours.

While Stacy and the wolves headed toward the fire, most of the forest animals were fleeing in the opposite direction. Stacy had never seen anything like it. As she and the pack swam across the lake, all kinds of animals paddled past them: beavers, otters, foxes, and even elk. Hundreds of birds soared overhead, flying away from the billowing smoke.

Stacy knew the animals were operating on instinct, protecting themselves from the smoke and the flames. Her instinct, however, and that of Page and her wolves, was to get to the other members of their pack as quickly as possible.

Stacy would never forgive herself if something had happened to Wink and Noah. It had been her decision to travel so far away without two members of the wolf pack. As they approached the taiga, dense smoke and ash filled the air, making Stacy's eyes water and her throat ache. But that was nothing compared to her fear that Wink and Noah might be in trouble.

How will we get to them without running into the fire ourselves? She could see that great swaths of the forest had already been burned. Cinders floated in the scorching air, dropping on the dry vegetation and sparking small blazes that could quickly become big. Each step was treacherous.

Suddenly Stacy saw what initially looked like the largest bird she'd ever seen flying toward the fire, accompanied by a loud humming sound.

"A helicopter!" Stacy yelled. She'd never seen one in person before. The noise confused her. It was also familiar to her. *But how?* She stopped in her tracks and stared up at the helicopter in the sky, mesmerized by its whirring noise. All of a sudden, Basil and Tucker pulled her behind some bushes. Everest was standing tall in front of her, baring his teeth at the helicopter above him.

"Uh, pretty sure it's going to help fight the fire, guys," Stacy said, stepping out from behind the bushes. "I don't need protecting from it, thanks. It's likely heading to where the fire is the most out of control. Hopefully that's not the cave."

A couple of bats flew past and hovered just over Page's head. That gave Stacy an idea. "Page, can the bats lead us to the cave?" she asked. "Show us the safest route?"

Page conferred with the bats for a moment and then gave Stacy a bark that sounded remarkably like yes.

"Find Wink and Noah," Stacy said.

Of course the bats had no control over the wind, but they were able to lead the pack through parts of the forest that were not being ravaged by the flames. Other areas were already so badly charred that there was nothing left to burn.

Those areas presented their own problems. The forest

was full of humans—humans who were dressed in suits that protected them from the tall flames, humans who wouldn't understand why a girl was racing *toward* a fire with a wolf pack, a dog, and a small colony of bats.

Stacy had never experienced a forest fire before, thankfully, but she had read about them. Still, she was shocked by the number of people who had shown up to fight the fire. She was grateful to them, of course, but they were making it particularly hard at the moment to run by unnoticed. They had to skirt a large campsite full of men and women in fire gear and others who seemed to be supporting them with water stations and a whole picnic table covered in radios, walkie-talkies, and cell phones. A group of people, their faces black with ash and soot, was gathered around a map, talking strategy. From what Stacy could see, parts of the map had been colored over with marker showing where the fire was most concentrated.

Stacy longed to get a look at the map, to see if their clearing and the cave were safe, but of course she couldn't do that without raising lots of questions.

Addison had the same thought. Stacy caught her just as she was about to run into the campsite and look at the map.

"No, Addi," Stacy whispered. "Too dangerous. Besides, Wink and Noah are smart." Addison shot her a look. "Well, Noah's smart at least. He'll have found a way to protect Wink and himself."

Stacy and the wolves were crouched in the undergrowth around the firefighters' campsite, trying to avoid notice and find the best route back to their cave. That was the first place she knew to look for Noah and Wink. If they had been forced to escape, they would have left some indication behind on the cave's map to let the others know where they had gone.

The firefighters were so close Stacy could hear their conversation.

"This is ground zero," one man said, pointing to a spot on his map.

"Careless campers?" asked another.

The first one shook his head. "Don't think so. But we did find some surveying equipment. The forest was so dry that any small spark could have set it off."

Stacy was about to try to slink off when she heard something that stopped her in her tracks. It was a woman's voice. Miriam.

"Could this have been arson? The pro-development groups?"

The man's face turned to stone. "That's a serious accusation," he yelled over all the other shouting that echoed throughout the forest. "But I wouldn't put it past them. People won't fight to save a burned forest in the same way they would one that's full of life. Probably easier to develop, too."

Stacy was so angry she nearly marched right up to the firefighters demanding to know what they would do about the developers. Everest nipped at her ankles, reminding her with his loving gray eyes that she needed to stay hidden.

"All right," she whispered to the wolves and Page. "Keep low and follow me. We've got to get to the cave."

Stacy and the group crouched low to the ground and started slinking away from the campsite.

"Hey, a wolf!" she heard someone yell. "Wolves! They're running *toward* the fire."

Stacy and the others began to sprint away, but Stacy could still hear the humans talking about them as they ran.

"Those looked like Arctic wolves, didn't they?" a second voice asked.

"You're losing it, Mack," the first voice said with a laugh. "You must have inhaled too much smoke."

Half an hour later, the group was nearing the cave. Sweat dripped down Stacy's face and her hands were raw from crawling. A trip through the forest that should have taken them minutes was taking forever. The fire was burning steadily to the south of them and to the west along the river. From what Stacy could tell, it had not yet made it to their cave and the ridge. Stacy couldn't get over how many humans had come to fight the fire and she was sure she'd been spotted several times already. There was nothing she could do to prevent it at this point and it accomplished nothing to dwell on it now. Plus, any humans who spotted her would likely avoid her—no one wanted to mess with four wolves.

They reached a section of the forest that had been burned. Seeing the charred black earth instead of trees and plants made Stacy's heart hurt. Wisps of smoke rose into the air. The skies had grown dark and Stacy couldn't tell if a storm was coming or if it was just the heavy smoke that was everywhere.

"Basil, if someone sees me now, they see me," Stacy said urgently. "We've got to hurry."

Basil understood. She crouched to let Stacy climb onto her back and they raced the rest of the way to the cave.

As they entered the clearing, Stacy stepped over a freshly dug trench of water.

"This must have been Noah," she said. "Smart."

Wink nearly knocked them over with relief and excitement. Noah came to the cave opening and ushered Stacy and the others into the cave. Stacy was not prepared for the sight that awaited her.

There in the cave was a menagerie of all the animals in the taiga that weren't fast enough to outrun the fire. Wink and Noah must have herded them into the cave for safety. There was the doe and her two fawns, a fox, a cluster of rabbits, squirrels and raccoons, and a pine marten. Stacy even saw a lynx pacing at the back of the cave. She'd only seen a lynx once before in the taiga.

"You're all safe here," Stacy said, especially to the smaller animals, including Fluff, who was eyeing the fox and lynx nervously. "You're welcome to stay here until the fire is out."

Stacy was so relieved that Wink and Noah were okay. She turned and gave them huge hugs. Then she fell to her knees, hungry and exhausted. Noah brought her a water bucket. Wink proudly rolled a new jar of peanut butter in her direction. She could barely mutter her thanks before drinking and eating her fill.

She finished quickly and was about to help Tucker, who was currently performing triage on the assortment of animals in the cave, when the bats started zooming around Page.

Page ran to the map, jumped, and pointed her nose to the ridge above the cave—the very spot where Stacy had first seen Page surrounded by the other wolf pack.

"The wild wolves?" Stacy asked.

Page yipped.

"The fire must have jumped onto the ridge," Stacy said to the others. "The other pack is in danger. Firefighters can't get up there. We need to warn them before the fire spreads to their den."

Everest bristled and the others simply stared at Stacy with a look that said, *It's not worth the risk.*

Are they right? Those wolves have caused all kinds of trouble for us. Do I really want risk my wolves' lives in a forest fire to try to save them?

But of course that's exactly what Stacy wanted to do. She couldn't do anything else and she knew her pack was capable.

"We have to at least try to rescue them," she said, looking each one of them in the eye. "Basil, Wink, Everest, you're the fastest. Addison, Tucker, and Noah stay here with Page and watch over these animals. There might be other animals that need to be brought inside for safety."

"Okay, so it's the four of us," Stacy said to Everest, Wink, and Basil, pulling her satchel over her head. "Let's go."

TWENTY

A LARGE PART of the switchback that led from the cave to the ridge above had been burned away, which made climbing easier, but it also meant there was thick smoke clogging the air. Stacy's already irritated throat began to feel like it had been scraped raw. It was a slow, steep climb but they finally made it. Wink was at Stacy's side the whole time, while Basil led the way and Everest walked behind her, making sure she didn't fall.

When they finally reached the top, Stacy saw why the other wolves were in trouble. Not only was the fire creeping up the ridge behind them, it was already raging in the old oak forest on the other side of the ravine and was moving fast in their direction.

They pushed on toward the wild wolves' den, barely able to see through the dark smoke. They had just reached the den when the fire seemed to jump right over the ravine with a roar that was almost deafening.

Stacy could just make out a couple of the youngest wolves nervously pacing, clearly itching to leave, but Dusky and the rest of her pack stood their ground.

The fire was so close. Nothing could make it safe now. A couple of glowing cinders floated by Stacy's face. The fire would be upon them at any moment.

"Convince her to leave, Everest!" Stacy yelled. "Try to make her understand!"

Everest ran up to Dusky. They had a tense exchange that lasted several seconds and then Everest turned away and ran back to Stacy. Dusky was standing firm, refusing to leave.

"It's not safe here!" Stacy shouted. She knew they couldn't understand her, but maybe they'd hear the desperation in her voice. "Come with us! We have a place where we'll all be protected from the fire."

Stacy waited for Dusky to make the right decision for her pack, but she refused to do anything other than stay. The rest of her wolves began to panic as the flames became visible over the tops of the trees. A few of them fled, but the majority of them stayed where they were. Some looked as if they wanted to go with Stacy and Everest, yet didn't want to disobey their alpha.

Basil and Wink stepped up, communicating something to the wolves that Stacy couldn't understand.

The wolves seemed unsure.

"We have a safe place!" Stacy continued. "We've guaranteed safety to a lot of different animals, so you have to agree not to hunt while you're with us. But the fire will be here any second and we'll all burn. You have to decide right now."

But the decision was taken from them. What was once a strong, towering oak cracked in two and toppled over, flames licking at its branches. It fell right in the middle of the wild pack, crushing several of its members. Stacy screamed, unsure of how many wolves had just been killed right in front of her. *Wolves are dying. I have to get my wolves out of here.*

"COME NOW!" she pleaded to Dusky over the flames.

The alpha looked over her shoulder to see three of her wolves running away—not toward Stacy and Everest, but down the ravine toward the mines.

Then Stacy saw them. The two wolf pups huddled together near the downed tree. Had they lost their parents?

Flames danced closer and closer. No matter what Dusky did now, Stacy and her wolves had to leave. Staying would mean certain death. Stacy ran over and scooped up the wolf pups, one in each arm, and turned toward the direction of the switchback. She paused to look over her shoulder. Dusky stood alone in front of her den. She was illuminated by the flames, and Stacy could see a large patch of dark red on the wolf's hind-quarters . . . blood. Dusky wasn't placing any weight on her back left leg. *She'd been shot!* "She can't walk!" Stacy shouted to her wolves. But it was too late to help her. The flames enveloped what was left of the den and consumed Dusky. *Oh, Dusky. Poor girl.*

There was no time to mourn the loss of Dusky and the others. They set off down the switchback back to the safety of their cave.

"You're going to be okay," Stacy whispered to the pups as storm clouds began to gather around them. "We're going to take care of you."

They reached the bottom of the ridge just as the first crack of thunder boomed and raindrops fell. This was a good, steady rain, the kind of rain that put out fires and fed the earth.

"This should keep the fire from spreading," Stacy said. "We're going to be fine."

Suddenly, there was a blinding flash and then a big boom. Stacy instinctively crouched low to the ground and tightened her grip on both of the pups. She smelled singed fur.

"Basil! No!" Stacy staggered to her feet and peered through the already dwindling rain at Basil, who was trying to stand up. The wolf had a jagged, bloody strike down the left side of her body. Basil had been struck by lightning!

Stacy ran to Basil's side. Wink and Everest were already there, helping her to stand. Basil was stunned but alive. She took a few wobbly steps and slumped over Everest, who bowed down to catch her. Wink helped position her over Everest's back. The helicopter suddenly appeared overhead and dropped a red substance over an unburned area of the taiga. Everest stood at Stacy's side, ever her protector, Basil lying motionless across his back.

"Let's go!" Stacy shouted over the strangely familiar whirring of the helicopter blades. And with that, Stacy and the wolves raced back to their cave.

The cave was oddly quiet given the number of animals that were currently occupying the small space. Everyone had settled down to wait out the fire. Tucker was already licking the new wolf pups all over like he was their mama. Noah was busying himself keeping their guests hydrated. Page was sitting just outside the cave, ready to receive any messages that might come through from the bats. Stacy walked over to Everest, who was standing guard over Basil. Wink was lying on the floor next to her. She'd passed out, probably from the pain, when they were on the way back to the cave. She hadn't woken up yet.

"How is she?" Stacy asked Everest. His sad silver eyes told Stacy that Basil's condition was not good. Stacy examined the jagged red line on her side from the lightning strike. "Once Noah's done getting everyone water, let's have him rinse off some of this blood. We've got to keep the wound clean. An infection is what could do her in, if she's not already bleeding internally."

Stacy walked over to the cave entrance. She was proud of herself that she'd managed to keep it together in front of Everest and Wink. On the inside, she was anything but calm. *Basil can't die. She just needs to make it through the night. If she can do that, then she should be able to pull through.*

The rain continued as night began to draw near. As far as Stacy could tell, peering out the cave entrance at the charred surroundings, the fire was extinguished. Suddenly, Stacy heard a muffled voice coming from the trees at the edge of the clearing.

"Better get inside, Page," Stacy said. But as she was turning to escort the dog inside, she saw Addison emerge from the trees where the voice had come from.

"Addi!" Stacy shouted in a hushed voice. "What are you doing? Get in here now!"

As Addison walked toward her, Stacy could see she had something in her mouth. The crackled voice rang out again. *It was coming from . . . Addison.*

"You. Stole. A. Walkie. Talkie?" Stacy grabbed the device from Addison's mouth. "You're a genius, Addison."

Stacy tuned the dial on the top of the walkie-talkie and held it up to her ear to try to make out what the voices were saying.

"We're gonna circle over the ridge once more to make sure, but the rain did most of the work for us. Fire's contained now. Over."

Stacy breathed a sigh of overwhelming relief. The fire wasn't all the way out, but the danger of it spreading was gone. One by one, the various animals in the cave left, bowing their heads in thanks to Stacy and the wolves as they exited. Soon the cave was empty again.

Tucker was at Basil's side, and Stacy knew he wouldn't sleep tonight. Everest had positioned himself at the cave entrance to stand guard for the night while Stacy took her usual spot with the wolves to sleep. She rested her head on Wink's back and let the wolf pups curl up against her stomach. Page curled up at her feet. Tucked between Addison and Noah, Stacy closed her eyes. But sleep did not come. The peace she usually felt nestled among the wolves was no longer there.

Did someone really start this fire intentionally? Is the taiga going to be turned into a golf course? Will the village roll back the wolf bounty now that most of Dusky's pack has perished in the fire? How many firefighters spotted me today? How many saw my wolves? Will they come looking for us? And why did the helicopter affect me the way it did?

Something about the sound of the blades had been so familiar to Stacy, but the memory was too wispy and far away to grasp. Like today, it was connected to smoke and burning . . . and. . . her parents.

A memory? I think it has to do with the part of the forest the wolves don't want me to explore . . . beyond where the moose was stuck.

There were too many questions circling around and around in her head, just like the helicopter she could not make sense of. But for all the uncertainty Stacy felt, there was one thing of which she was absolutely sure. She was more determined than ever to protect her wolves, defend the taiga, and find the answers to her all of these questions, even if it meant interacting more with humans. Stacy stared up at the cave ceiling at peace with her new mission. One of the wolf pups yawned and turned over.

Things are about to change around here, that's for certain. But it will have to wait until tomorrow.

arson—a crime where someone seeks to destroy a property by setting it on fire. Example: *The forest fire could have been an act of arson.*

balked—to hesitate or stubbornly refuse when asked to do something. Example: *Everest balked when Stacy told him she wanted to enter the abandoned mineshaft.*

conglomeration—an unexpected combination of things. Example: *Stacy's chicken, apple, and pumpkin stew was a strange conglomeration.*

crepuscular—related to the twilight hours of the day. Sometimes used to describe an animal that is most active at daybreak and dusk. Example: *The wolves were crepuscular, so naturally they woke Stacy up at dawn to go adventuring in the forest.*

culled—to reduce the amount of something, often a population of animals by hunting. Example: *Dusky's pack was being culled and there was nothing Stacy or her wolves could do about it.*

diminutive—exceptionally small. Example: *Standing between Tucker's legs was a diminutive, snarling red fox.*

disdain—a dislike or lack of respect for something or someone. Example: *The campers' careless disdain for the forest did come in handy time and time again.*

entwined—to become twisted or weaved together. Example: *The moose's antlers were so tightly entwined in the vines that the poor thing couldn't even lower its head to drink.*

formidable—impressively large; causing admiration or intimidation due to one's physical size. Example: *Everest was as formidable as the mountain he was named after.*

gauging—to measure or estimate the outcome of something, such as a decision. Example: *Wink was gauging if he could make the jump over the magma and back with the dog.*

lichen—a simple and crust-like plant that grows on top of walls, trees, and rocks. Example: *Basil had slowed down enough that the individual trees and the grayish-green lichen on their trunks came into focus.*

menagerie—an unusual assortment of animals. Example: *There in the cave was a menagerie of all the animals in the taiga that weren't fast enough to outrun the fire.*

pelage—a mammal's fur, hair, or wool. Example: *Stacy buried her head in the thick pelage of Basil's neck.*

permeated—to spread through or infiltrate something. Example: *The scorching sulfur smell permeated every inch of them when they were deep in the cave.*

perpetual—constant or unending. Example: *Stacy called that dark area the Forest of Perpetual Darkness.*

proclivity—a tendency or talent for doing something. Example: *Addison was curiously clever for a wolf and had a proclivity for arithmetic.*

rambunctious—uncontrollably energetic. Example:

Page obeyed Everest and Basil on the rare instances she got too rambunctious.

ravenous—extreme hunger. Example: *Everest pushed a piece of bread toward her lips and Stacy realized she was ravenous.*

reposing—in a state of rest or relaxation. Example: *After everyone had finished their dinner, Stacy cleaned and put away their bowls and turned to face the sleepy, reposing pack.*

Rube Goldberg—a complex or intricate machine that accomplishes a simple task. Example: *The Dog Decider was a rather rustic Rube Goldberg machine Addison and Stacy had built together.*

sidled—to carefully approach something or someone, especially from the side. Example: *Basil, slender and athletic, emerged from the trees and sidled up beside Stacy.*

surmised—to come to a conclusion with limited evidence. Example: *Stacy surmised that Crow and the baby chicks had been eaten by the wild wolves.*

taiga—a northern subarctic forest primarily composed of coniferous trees including pine, fir, and spruce. Example: *Stacy had no idea how she'd come to live in the taiga with six Arctic wolves.*

theodolite—an instrument used for surveying land, particularly for measuring horizontal and vertical angles. Example: *Stacy fought the sudden urge to run out from behind the tree and kick over the theodolite.*

triage—the process of sorting through patients to determine who needs care most urgently. Example: *Tucker was performing triage on the assortment of animals in the cave.*

wafted—a smell that is carried through the air. Example: *In summer, the cool breezes in the forest wafted over Stacy and the wolves as they slept in the cave.*

FIELD TRIP TO THE TAIGA!

After the ocean, the taiga (or boreal forest) is the world's largest biome! It exists mostly in Canada and Russia, but there's also a small part in the United States, in northern Minnesota in Superior National Forest.

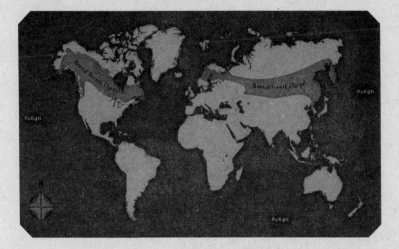

That's where Stacy traveled for the first three episodes of her YouTube series, *Minecraft Field Trips*, and where she got a lot of inspiration for the first book in the Wild Rescuers series!

She was able to fly in a helicopter over the forest, meet a real wolf pack at the International Wolf Center in Ely, Minnesota, and take a tour of the Soudan iron mines. She also got up close and personal with the real-life versions of items from Minecraft like podzol, mushrooms, and iron ore! You can follow her adventures on her YouTube channel: www.YouTube.com/StacyPlays.

The author in a helicopter while filming her Minecraft Field Trips *series.*

MEET THE REAL-LIFE PAGE!

Stacy adopted Page from a golden retriever sanctuary in West Virginia in 2007. Her name was spelled "Page" on the veterinary records and Stacy loved it and decided to keep it. Stacy has always said Page has more qualities of a wild fox than a dog. She is incredibly smart and knows over a dozen commands and tricks. Stacy often jokes that she can speak in full sentences to her and Page understands her.

Breed: Unknown, although she looks like a Pomeranian-shepherd mix
Age: Unknown (approximately 12 years old)
Rescue date: April 28, 2007
Favorite activity: Walking (or running) in a forest
Favorite foods: Salmon, asparagus (really!), and cheese
Fun fact: Page has been on an airplane with Stacy over 17 times!

The wolves in *Wild Rescuers: Guardians of the Taiga* are completely fictional, but while Stacy was researching this book in Ely, Minnesota, she was able to meet and interview Saranda Oestreicher, who has lots of experience interacting with real wolves in the wild.

Saranda "collaring" a wolf. A mask is used to protect its eyes.

Name:
Saranda Oestreicher

Current job / past job:
Currently, I am a fish and wildlife technician with the 1854 Treaty Authority. Previously, I worked at the International Wolf Center.

Why do you love wolves?
I've felt an undeniable connection to wolves ever since I was a child; I grew up in awe of them and knew I had to pursue a career studying them. Wolves are so adaptable, hardy, and loyal to their packs. My curiosity about wolves never dulls.

What IS your job?
Most of my time right now is spent collaring wolves in northern Minnesota. I also study moose, loons, various carnivores, and a variety of fish species.

What type of wolves do you work with?
I currently work with gray wolves, specifically the Great Plains subspecies.

What is the greatest threat facing wolves?
Overall, humans. Threats range from indirect problems like habitat reduction, to direct causes such as killing wolves. To this day, there are still many common misconceptions, myths, and much folklore about wolves that definitely have an impact.

What is the coolest wildlife encounter you've had?
Definitely when I collared my first wolf pups! We had an adult male collared in the pack and we weren't sure if he was the breeding male, so we didn't know if we'd even find the den site. Eventually, we came up to a picture-perfect meadow full of sunshine. While we were looking for the den, all of a sudden we saw a pile of seven pups under a tree napping! We accidentally woke them up and they all scurried back to the den. I had never see wild wolf pups before and that day I tagged the whole litter. A month or two later, I was going out to check the radio signals of those pups and they ran across the trail in front of me and it was the best feeling ever to see them again.

What other animals have you seen during your time in the wilderness?

I have seen a lot of wildlife during work or during personal time while hiking and/or camping. I worked in Wyoming collaring mule deer fawns and I saw a lot of amazing wildlife out there as well. I've also backpacked across Europe while I was an undergraduate and got the opportunity to view some European wildlife! Overall, just to name a few, I've seen: wolves, grizzly bears, black bears, mule deer, elk, pronghorn antelope, moose, golden eagles, peregrine falcons, bald eagles, white-tailed deer, roe deer and red deer (in Europe), and bobcats.

What advice do you have for people who want to do what you do?

Learn. Enjoy learning. Start volunteering, go to college, volunteer as much as you can, gain experience, and then go to graduate school. Even if you want to focus on one niche of the field, make sure to gain experiences in a variety of studies. Those experiences will make you well rounded and adaptable. Most of all: be curious and have passion. Find what lights a fire in your heart and never stop working toward that goal. Be diligent, smart, and hardworking. Combine your passion with your brains and you'll be unstoppable.

ACKNOWLEDGMENTS

Thank you to my dad for being my biggest cheerleader and helping me in more ways than I could ever acknowledge. I'd be lost without you. Thank you to my mom for reading to me, filling my head with big words, for color walks, Mothra pancakes, introducing me to Harry Potter, and always making sure I had a library card even during the years I read nothing but Archie Double Digests.

Thank you to my editor, Sara Sargent. You are the best. Thank you for being so patient with me and for bringing this book to life. I'm so lucky to work with you. Thank you Colleen O'Connell for bringing me into the HarperCollins family in the first place. Margot Wood, thank you for being such an amazing friend, confidante, and for your marketing expertise.

To the rest of the HarperCollins team—a massive thank-you to Meaghan Finnerty, Olivia Russo, Nellie Kurtzman, Kerry Moynagh, and Kathy Faber. Andrea

Pappenheimer for your infectious enthusiasm for the project and confidence in me. And, of course, a special thanks to Kate Jackson and Suzanne Murphy.

Thank you also to Laurie Calkhoven and Jacqueline Hornberger for guiding me through my first experience turning in a manuscript. Vivienne To for bringing my characters to life in the most beautiful way. And Alison Klapthor and Jessie Gang for their impeccable aesthetic. I felt so safe in your competent hands.

To my Minecraft family: Joey, Lizzie, Stampy, Sqaishey, AmyLee, Aureylian, Graser, Meghan, Jaspanda, PDawg, Nathan (and his mom!). To my friends Tiffany and Mario for their excellent advice and friendship. To my manager at YouTube, Meg Campbell, thank you for everything.

To Lydia Winters, Vu Bui, and all the folks at Mojang and Microsoft who work tirelessly on the game that has taken over my life for the past five years and fueled my obsession with pixelated wolves. Saranda Oestreicher for answering my ridiculous questions about actual wolves so there would be some semblance of reality in this book. And Andy Rosenberg, thank you for your friendship and keeping me sane.

And last, thank you to my YouTube viewers. You've

made this all possible and I hope you enjoy this new chapter in the world of Dogcraft. Page and Molly love you; go rescue a dog!

The adventure continues in

WILD RESCUERS: ESCAPE TO THE MESA

Read on for a sneak peek!

ONE

LICK.

Lick.

Lick.

A smile crept across Stacy's face as the small dog nuzzled her awake.

"Hi, Page," Stacy said groggily.

It was strangely cold in the cave. Stacy opened her eyes, instantly aware that she and Page were alone.

Typically, Stacy slept nestled among her pack of Arctic wolves, their soft white fur providing Stacy with more warmth than any blanket or comforter ever could. And usually, the wolves waited for Stacy to wake up. But this morning was different. Her wolves were gone.

Panic began to bubble up inside of her as she frantically rubbed her eyes and looked around until she spotted them. They weren't gone at all; they just weren't cuddled beside her. Everest, the alpha of the pack, was guarding the entrance to the cave. He was exchanging looks with Tucker, who was also at the cave entrance. Stacy remembered that last night had been Tucker's turn to do patrol duty on the ridge. He must have just returned to update Everest on the evening's events.

Basil, the beta of the pack, was curled up by the cave's hearth, where a healthy fire was crackling. *Silly Basil,* Stacy thought to herself. *She survives being struck by lightning and yet she still likes to start fires.* Addison, the pack's other female wolf, was sitting near the large spruce table in the cave where Stacy prepared the pack's meals and did various crafting projects. Behind her, Noah splashed in the small freshwater spring that flowed through the back of their cave. That was all her wolves accounted for—all except . . .

"Where's Wink?" Stacy asked, sitting up. *He shouldn't be out by himself.* The fire that had spread through the taiga a couple of months before had driven all the hunters away for a while, but Stacy suspected there might still be a bounty on the wolves. Which meant they could all be in danger.

Suddenly, Wink came bounding into the cave. At least, Stacy was pretty sure it was Wink. It was hard to tell because his normally brilliant white fur was brown, as if he'd been rolling in dirt. His front paws were completely covered in mud, which he was now tracking into the cave. Everest growled quietly in dismay at the mess. Wink sauntered up to Stacy and innocently dropped a mouthful of crumpled peonies on her lap.

Stacy blinked a couple of times and looked at the pink flowers. They were covered in slobber and were already beginning to wilt. It was almost like Wink had dug them up in the forest days ago and then buried them until this morning. Actually, that was exactly what it was like. But why?

What is going on? Stacy thought. *First my wolves are all up and about without me. Now these flowers?* And then it hit her. Today must be the eighth day of October. Today was her "rescue day."

Since no one knew when Stacy's birthday was, they'd celebrated her rescue day every year since she'd come to live with the wolves in the taiga forest. This was year number five. Every morning of her rescue day, each wolf would give Stacy a gift to mark the occasion. How the wolves kept track of which day it was, Stacy hadn't a clue. Nor was she sure of the exact details of the events that led to her being rescued and taken in by six Arctic wolves in the first place.

Any memories Stacy had of those events were buried deep in her mind. No matter how hard she tried, she couldn't remember anything. It wasn't like she could ask the wolves. Over the years, the group had developed their own way of communicating with each other through barks, facial expressions, and body language, but they couldn't talk or write—although Stacy was convinced that Addison was trying to learn how to read.

"Thank you, Wink," Stacy said, picking up the flowers and cradling them in her arms. "These were . . . uh, I mean, these *are* beautiful."

Wink stared up at her expectantly. "Oh, you're right, I didn't smell them," Stacy said as she brought the droopy blooms up to her nose. "Mmm. So sweet." She set the flowers down beside her. Page sniffed them and immediately buried her nose in her paws.

Stacy stood and walked across the cave to her rocking chair and took a seat. She knew what was coming next. One by one the other wolves were going to bring her a gift.

Sure enough, Tucker was already making his way toward her, dragging something behind him. Stacy leaned out of her rocking chair, craning her neck. As soon as she saw what it was, she let out a tiny gasp and stood up. Tucker was bringing her a large bow and a quiver filled with arrows. He pulled it as far as Stacy's feet and then looked up at her nervously, waiting to see if Stacy would be happy about being gifted a weapon on her rescue day.

"Wow," Stacy said reverently, crouching to the cave floor and running her fingers along the bow. "Tucker, how did you get this?"

Tucker's rust-colored eyes danced around the cave. It wasn't like Tucker to steal from people who came into the taiga. But if there was one thing Tucker hated, it was hunting. He must have swiped it from a hunter knowing Stacy would only use it for good. And with everything that happened over the summer with the wolf bounty, including the time when Dusky, the alpha of the wild wolf pack, was shot, Stacy was grateful to have another way to protect herself and the pack besides her small knife.

"Thank you, Tuck," Stacy said. "I'll have to practice a lot, but I'm glad you brought me this. For now, though, why don't you put it on my desk over there . . . out of Page's reach."

Tucker eagerly obliged, pulling the bow and quiver of

arrows onto the flat boulder Stacy used as a desk. Then Addison took a step toward Stacy and pointed her snout toward the crafting table, where a pumpkin pie, Stacy's favorite, was cooling. Addison had baked it by the fire in an old tin they'd found at a campsite. Stacy knew wolves weren't supposed to know mathematics, but Addison did (another reason why Stacy suspected she knew how to read). That knowledge made the graceful wolf particularly proficient in things like baking, where exact measurements were required.

"Addi, that smells delicious, thank you," Stacy said, sitting back down in her chair. Addison beamed with pride.

Next was Noah, who had walked over while Stacy had been examining the bow. He proudly presented Stacy with some wet clay he'd fished up from the river banks.

"Thanks, boy," Stacy said, turning the soft clay over in her hands. She looked at Wink. "We can use this to make a flowerpot. Then the next time you bring me peonies they won't die so quickly."

Wink wagged his tail and Stacy gave both him and Noah a pat on their heads.

Stacy got out of her chair and walked over to a sullen-looking Basil. The scar from where Basil had been struck by lightning during July's thunderstorm was almost healed. New fur was beginning to grow in where the worst burns had been. After the fire, Stacy and the wolves had spent the rest of the summer lying low in the cave and caring for Basil.

The lightning strike had seemed to affect Basil more on the inside than the outside. It had weakened her and she'd had to learn to walk all over again. She was able to walk short distances now, but was in no shape to leave the cave to find Stacy a present.

"The best gift you could *ever* give me is to get better, girl," Stacy said, kneeling down beside her and gently cupping Basil's muzzle in her hands. "I mean that."

Basil stared up at Stacy, her giant yellow eyes finding Stacy's emerald green ones. Stacy kissed Basil's head and turned to look at Everest, who had appeared next to her in front of the fire. His silver eyes bore a serious expression.

"Everest," Stacy started. "It's okay if you didn't get me anything either, I . . ."

Stacy's voice trailed off as she noticed Everest was holding something in his jaw. He lowered his head to where Stacy's hands were. She turned her palms up and he dropped the small item into them.

Stacy stared blankly at the object in her hands. It

felt . . . familiar. It was a small silver charm bracelet. Stacy squinted her eyes, hoping that the memory attached to the bracelet would somehow come into focus.

She examined the charms; they had a dirty gray patina to them. There was a horse, a book, a helicopter, a letter S, and a mermaid.

"Everest," Stacy whispered. "Where did you get this?"

She looked up at Everest, who had a sad, wistful expression on his face.

Stacy knew, of course, that he couldn't answer her. Still, she waited to see if Everest would make some gesture to give her a clue about where the bracelet came from. Instead, he walked past Stacy and lay down next to Basil. Stacy frowned for a moment. *Why is he acting so odd?*

"Thank you, everyone," Stacy said, turning to address the entire pack. "You've made this the best rescue day ever."

The wolves looked around at each other, obviously pleased with themselves.

Stacy retreated to the back of the cave to change out of her pajamas and into her everyday clothes—a pair of worn blue jeans and her favorite blue-and-white-striped long-sleeved T-shirt. The shirt was incredibly soft from years of wear. Sometimes Stacy had to stop herself from sleeping in it, too. She didn't want to wear it out too fast—she and Addison had already sewn patches onto both of the threadbare elbows, which had ripped open during their last animal rescue—a small pine marten who had injured its leg. Tucker had devised an ingenious splint for it using a discarded tent stake which he'd affixed onto the little mammal with some moss and tree sap that would likely break away after a few weeks of healing.

Stacy walked over to her little makeshift bookcase in the cave and set the charm bracelet down on one of the shelves. She couldn't quite put her finger on it, but something about Everest's body language made Stacy think he hadn't just found it in the woods. The bracelet felt so familiar. She was sure she had seen it before. *Why can't I remember where?*

She looked up at the top of the bookcase, where her pet chicken, Fluff, roosted. Stacy reached her hand under Fluff and pulled out a speckled egg. Digging her hand into her pants pocket, she pulled out a handful of seeds.

"Here's your breakfast, girl," Stacy said, patting her feathers. "Thank you for mine."

Stacy walked across the cave and set the egg down in front of Addison, who was tidying up as Wink and Page chased each other around the crafting table.

"I'm going to scramble that when I get back, okay?" Stacy said to Addison, walking over to the cave entrance and peering outside. It was drizzling, but she could see through the mist and clouds that the sun was just coming up over the giant spruce trees to the east.

"We're late," Stacy said to the pack, pulling on her leather boots. She tied the right one up while Everest, carefully holding the laces in his teeth, tied the left. Stacy stood and grabbed her old leather satchel that hung on a hook near the cave entrance. She turned around to see Everest and Basil waiting for her command.

"Okay, let's go," she said. "You too, Page. Droplet and Splat will be expecting us."

Check out the Wild Rescuers series by

Stacy Plays